P
CHAS

D0000471

"A wonderful, tough, and totally believable story about brutality, resilience, friendship under fire, and the healing power of athletics. Hang on tight. This is quite a ride."

—Chris Crutcher, author of *Angry Management*

"I love *Chasing AllieCat*. It's proof again of what a tremendous writer Becky Davis is: smart, touching, and generous in spirit. She creates in Sadie, Allie, Joe, Siren, and these other characters a magnificent group of survivors that everyone will love getting to know!"

—Terry Trueman, author of the
Michael L. Printz Award-winning novel,
Stuck in Neutral

"Dangerous."

—Terry Davis, author of *Vision Quest*

Also by Rebecca Fjelland Davis

Jake Riley: Irreparably Damaged

CHASING
ALLIECAT

For Alexander

REBECCA FJELLAND DAVIS

Woodbury, Minnesota

First Edition
First Printing, 2011

Book design by Steffani Sawyer
Cover design by Lisa Novak
Cover image of cyclists © 2010 iStockphoto.com/Nazreen Essack
           forest © 2010 iStockphoto.com/Pawel Gaul

Flux, an imprint of Llewellyn Worldwide Ltd.

This is a work of fiction. Names, characters, places, and incidents are either the product of the author's imagination or are used fictitiously, and any resemblance to actual persons (living or dead), business establishments, events, or locales is entirely coincidental.

Library of Congress Cataloging-in-Publication Data
Davis, Rebecca Fjelland.
   Chasing AllieCat / Rebecca Fjelland Davis.—1st ed.
      p. cm.
   Summary: When she is left with relatives in rural Minnesota for the summer, Sadie meets Allie, a spiky-haired off-road biker, and Joe, who team up to train for a race, but when they find a priest badly beaten and near death in the woods, Allie mysteriously disappears, leaving Sadie and Joe to discover the dangerous secret she is hiding.
   ISBN 978-0-7387-2130-9
   [1. Family problems—Fiction. 2. Mountain biking—Fiction. 3. Violence—Fiction. 4. Interpersonal relations—Fiction. 5. Grief—Fiction. 6. Minnesota—Fiction.] I. Title. II. Title: Chasing Allie Cat.
   PZ7.D2977Ch 2011
   [Fic]—dc22

                                        2010038217

Flux
Llewellyn Worldwide Ltd.
2143 Wooddale Drive
Woodbury, MN 55125-2989
www.fluxnow.com

Printed in the United States of America

In Gratitude…

To all the guys who let me draft behind them for hundreds and hundreds of miles: the real Mike Busch of the real A-1 Bike, Skarpohl, TerryB, Grumpy Tom, Big Brian, Mini Brian, Dan the Ironman, Matt B, Rio, and Danny; and to all my other cycling friends: Bill, Heidi, Tim, Lisa, Steve, Rachael, David, Danielle, Daryl, Jeanne, Renee, John, Jann, Brian, Charlie, Brady, Jenna, Justin, and many more who make riding so much fun; and to John Anderson, who first made me believe I could be a serious cyclist.

To George Nicholson, for believing in me through thick and thin, to Brian Farrey, Sandy, Courtney, Steve, and the wonderful Flux folk who believe in this story; to Steve Deger, who believed in Sadie and Allie and Joe when almost nobody else did; to the Tatas, Sisters in Ink, for reading and believing; and to Tom, for understanding tunnel vision.

And most of all, to my kids, who always believe.

Like dogs, bicycles are social catalysts
that attract a superior category of people.

—Chip Brown, *A Bike and a Prayer*

Finding Father

July 1

AllieCat disappeared the day we found Father Malcolm.

Allie and Joe and I were charging our mountain bikes through the junk woods like we always did, bouncing over ruts and tree limbs and sand hills. The night before, a thunderstorm had blasted through Blue Earth County. Tree branches were down all over the place and wet leaves plastered the ground. We rode around the trailer park cemetery—where Mr. Turtle, the trailer court landlord, buries dead trailers, not people—and we slid up and down hills slick as ice with the wet green leaves. Allie headed down the big steep slope to the Blue Earth River, but behind her, Joe froze at the top of the hill.

Joe does that on hills. At the top of the hill, he hit his brakes, which is what you *don't* do when you're riding a bike on a slippery surface, whether it's snow or loose gravel or loose sand or wet leaves. You follow the flow of your front tire, but you don't slam on your brakes.

Joe slammed.

"Stay off the brakes!" I yelled. "Go. Just ride through it. Let go and follow your front wheel."

Joe let go of his brakes and started down the incline.

"Steer into the slide," Allie hollered from down the hill, ahead of us. "Just feather your brakes!"

But Joe couldn't stay off the brakes.

He made it about fifteen feet down the hill, fishtailing all over the place, and then went down. His shoulder smacked into the ground and he zipped downward in the wet leaves like he and his bike were sideways on a water slide.

His handlebar hooked a cedar sapling beside the trail, and his bike swung around it like a yo-yo. Joe catapulted over the edge of the ravine and shot out into space, skimming scraggly treetops and yelling to beat the band, and then disappearing, trailing his "Aaaaahhhh..." through the air behind him.

"Pussy!" Allie screamed over her shoulder from the bottom of the hill. But she'd braked and looked back just in time to see Joe fly out of sight. That shut her up.

I guided my front wheel down the hill about ten feet behind Joe. I tapped my brakes lightly to slow down some more, but my back tire slid out from under me anyway, and wet green rushed at me. I smacked down on my side and I felt my shoulder and my helmet bounce. I kicked like crazy and twisted my feet so my shoes unclipped from my pedals as I slid. I grabbed for dirt, mud, leaves, anything to stop sliding. My foot found a root and I stopped just before the edge of the ravine.

Allie, stopped at the bottom of the hill, struggled to unclip from her pedals and yelled, "Sadie! Joe! You guys okay?"

"Fine," I yelled. I scrambled to my feet, brushed off wet leaves.

"Holy crap!" Joe hollered from somewhere below us. "Holy crap! Get down here *quick*!"

"What!?" I yelled, moving toward his voice. "You okay?"

"Why don't you just swear and get it over with," Allie yelled. "I'm so sick of hearing you say *holy crap*."

"Just get down here, then!" Joe's voice cracked. "Oh, crap! Hurry up!"

"Are you hurt?" I moved over the edge of the ravine, working to keep my footing, and then approached Joe in leaps. He had landed against the only decent-sized tree trunk on the steep slope. He sat there, leaning on the scraggly fir tree that had kept him from falling the last twenty feet, and stared toward the bottom of the ravine.

"Look," he said.

I looked.

The first thing I saw was his bike, still in one piece, at the bottom of the hill. Next to it, a ripped blue plastic tarp was spread over the ground. Joe pointed. Two brown shoes, toes down, soles up, lay in the mud, sticking out from under the plastic sheet. There were feet in the shoes, attached to legs that disappeared under the tarp.

"Holy crap," Joe said again.

"I am so sick," said Allie, scrambling down to us, "of your '*holy crap.*' I wish—" She saw the feet. "Oh, Christ!" We looked at each other and back at the feet. Then she almost managed a crooked grin. "Lost soles."

I tried to smile at her perverse joke, but my mouth wouldn't bend that way. It was hard enough just to breathe, much less smile. It was harder to get air in my lungs just then than it was riding up Embolism Hill following Allie's wheel.

"Do you think," Joe croaked, "he's dead?"

"Only one way to find out," Allie said, picking her way down to the tarp.

"Think we should just leave him be and go call the cops?" Joe said, struggling to his feet.

"Good idea." I nodded and backed farther away from the tarp and the feet. I could feel my breakfast rising inside me.

"Either way," Joe said, "dead or alive, we've got to call the cops." He glared at Allie's back. "Wish I had my cell phone. But of course—"

Allie cut him off with a shrug. "So we have to *go* call. I'll go."

"If he's alive…" I croaked, my mouth sandpapery, realizing that my voice had to filter through my fingers because I couldn't seem to peel my hand away from my mouth. "If he's still alive, a few minutes can make a lot of difference. You know, CPR and all that… He could die while we're getting help."

"I don't know about you," Allie said, "but I'm not doin' CPR on *that*…"

"Too bad," Joe said again, "that it's such a *crime* to carry a cell phone."

Allie threw him a black look. It was easy to picture the day Joe had answered his phone while we were on a ride, and Allie had left him in the dust and said she wouldn't ride with him if he brought it along anymore—"If you can't go without civilization, stay home."

Allie stepped toward the tarp.

This morning, Joe had remembered at the last minute, and I'd watched him fish his phone out of his jersey pocket and toss it on the driver's seat of his car before we went to meet Allie.

Allie leaned over the tarp. "We gotta see if he's dead."

Joe and I crept behind her, as if the guy would jump up at us. Maybe it was a ploy; he had hidden under the tarp and he'd come roaring to life, brandishing a tree branch— or a gun. We all must have been thinking the same thing because Joe jerked a stick, bigger than a baseball bat, out of the wet leaves. "Here." He handed it to me. "Hold this, just in case."

I nodded, grabbed the end of the stick, and moved into position as if I were stepping into the batter's box—a space within hitting distance of the body.

Allie nudged one leg with her foot. The leg didn't budge. Joe lifted a corner of the tarp. No response. He lifted higher so we could see all the way to the body's waist. The legs lay inside mud-smeared navy Dockers.

A look of steel determination came over Allie's face, like when she pumps up a hill on her bike. She took the opposite corner and flung it off the guy. His head, mostly nose-down in the mud, was turned toward Allie. She stepped closer and bent to look at the face.

Then Allie sucked air so hard, it sounded like somebody punched her. She stumbled backwards and grabbed her stomach. "Oh my God! It's Father Malcolm."

"Who?" I said, lowering my club.

"Is … he … dead?" she whispered.

He—the Father Whoever guy—wore a black priest's shirt, still tucked into the navy Dockers in a few places. Otherwise, the shirt hung out. His arms lay skewed at awkward angles, one up and one down, bent in places where there were no joints. Mud caked his gray hair. There was blood everywhere, on his shoulders, dried on both sides of his head, crusted on the clerical shirt collar.

"Who?" I asked again.

"Father Malcolm."

"A priest?" I said. "This is the priest you know?"

"You know this guy?" Joe asked. "How? Who is he?"

"He's a priest." Allie stood, hugging her rib cage.

"That much I figured," Joe said.

"Is he dead?" Allie asked again.

Joe squatted down beside him, braver now that he knew the guy wasn't a mugger. "He stinks."

"Yeah," I said, tossing the stick into the weeds. I squatted beside Joe and clapped my hand back over my mouth and nose. "But he stinks like blood and piss. Not like a dead animal. Does he have a pulse?"

Joe peeled the biking glove off his right hand and stuffed it in his jersey pocket.

"Hurry up!" Allie said, squatting on the other side of him.

Through my hand again, I said, "He could die while we're staring at him."

"*You* wanna check his pulse?" Joe hissed at me. "Be my guest."

"I'll shut up," I said.

Joe took a deep breath and extended his hand like he would to a poisonous snake.

He picked up the wrist and the hand hung limp. The fingers and fingernails were full of mud. But there was no blood there. "He's still warm," Joe said. He put his fingers on the inside of the wrist. He shifted his grip, and shifted it again. His eyes were on the treetop, eyebrows scrunched in concentration while he searched for a pumping artery. "There! Yeah. He's *alive*!" Joe grinned, triumphant, as if he'd saved him. "You wanna feel it?"

"You outta your mind?" I shrank backward, slipped in the mud, and fell onto my butt.

Allie leaned over. "Father Malcolm? Can you hear us?" She grabbed his shoulder and wiggled it. "Father Malcolm!" She straightened up, her face pale. Until that moment, I'd thought she was fearless. Guess I was wrong. "We gotta get an ambulance," she said.

"Cell phone," Joe said.

Allie whirled at him. "All right already," she yelled into his face. "So I was wrong! So you should have brought it. *I'll* go call 911 from the *Clark* Station down the hill." She turned and sprinted back toward her bike before Joe or I could argue.

"*How* do you know this priest?" I hollered at her backside.

"I'm gone," Allie shouted back. Out of sight, she added, "I'll tell them where to find you."

"You'll probably have to lead 'em here," Joe yelled back. "Hurry up!"

No answer.

And that was the last we saw of AllieCat.

ONE

Cannonballs Fly

May 28

My summer had started with a bang. That was the day I met Allie.

Mom and Dad are divorced, but sort of friends. Dad is an anthropology professor at the University of Minnesota. He was spending his sabbatical year in Egypt, doing Nefertiti research. He called mom and told her she should come to Egypt for the summer, that she'd love it.

At first she said, "Absolutely not. Are you crazy? Because that's what a divorce *means.*"

She didn't know I was listening to her half of the conversation, and she asked Dad, "Sid, isn't *she* in Amarna with you?"

"Does Dad have a girlfriend?" I asked Mom later.

"He *did.*"

When he called me the next weekend, I asked him, "Dad, do you have a girlfriend?"

"Not anymore, Sadie," he said.

"Who was she?" I asked. "How come I never met her?"

"A Ph.D. student. She came with me to do research, but we drove each other nuts. We can't work together. She went back to Minneapolis."

"So now you want Mom back?"

"Sadie, don't get your hopes up. It doesn't mean we're getting back together. But your mother and I work well together. And she'd love it here. She'd *thrive.*"

Well, God forbid I should stand in the way of my own mother *thriving.* Talk about a guilt trip if I complained about getting ditched for the summer while my parents were in *Africa.* I did, anyway—complain, that is—but then I thought they might get back together, so I quit whining and packed for the summer at Uncle Scout's.

✖✖

Mom had her ticket for Cairo in her bag when we showed up—mom, my eight-year-old brother Timmy, and me, suitcases and my mountain bike loading down her Subaru Forester, which she let me drive for once—for the traditional Memorial Day picnic at Scout and Susan's house in LeHillier, Minnesota, a township within the city limits of Mankato. And let me tell you, LeHillier is the armpit of America.

Mom's whole extended family—Scout and Susan and their four kids, Grandma, Mom's other brother Thomas and his wife Janie and two kids—were all at Scout's. They were waiting for us so they could start eating.

For dessert, Mom passed around her famous peanut butter pie. "Can't tell you thanks enough, Scout and Susan, for letting Sadie and Timmy stay here all summer."

Susan bit her lip and looked at Scout. Uncle Scout bellowed, "Absolutely dee-lighted to have them." He winked at me.

Susan looked at her lap. Finally she took a bite of pie and looked at me as if she was seeing me for the first time. "Sadie, would you mind babysitting sometimes?"

I looked at Mom. The truth was yes, I would mind. I'd mind a lot. But that would be an anti-mom-*thriving* kind of thing to say. I looked around at Stevie sitting next to Timmy, at Megan, at little Josie in her booster chair, and at Stacie crammed into her highchair, food all over the place. I breathed out. And I said, "I can babysit, but I have to get a job this summer. And I need to ride my bike every day."

Aunt Janie looked at Aunt Susan and said sideways to me, "You *need* to ride your bike? You may think you *need* a job, but riding your bike isn't something a person *needs*—"

"I want to start mountain-bike racing this year, so yeah. I *need* to." I'd been too chicken to race so far. This year, I was determined to do it, and Mom knew it. I looked at her to back me up. I didn't mind making her feel a little bit guilty about ditching us for the summer.

Mom gave me that *please work with me here* look, and I shot back a look that said I hoped *my* thriving mattered to her a tiny little bit, too. She played the diplomat. "Seems like you'd have time for all three. And this *is* the perfect location to mountain bike."

I looked back at Aunt Susan and let out a sigh. On purpose. To be a bit dramatic. It wasn't my fault we needed a place to stay, after all—it was Mom's—but I was the one who had to pay. I also knew I could make it worse or I could cooperate, but I didn't feel much like cooperating. "I can babysit. Some." I looked down. "I mean, sure. Yes."

Aunt Janie looked at me and said to Aunt Susan, "And I'm sure both Sadie and Timmy can help you in your big garden, too."

"Good idea," Aunt Susan said, giving me the first smile of the day. "You can both help Stevie and Megan and me in the garden."

I tried not to glare at Aunt Janie.

My little brother Timmy, who couldn't think of anything more exciting than spending the summer with his cousin Stevie, said, "I can work in the garden!"

And so, my fate was sealed.

LeHillier was going to cut me off from my entire world. I'd just turned sixteen on May 23, so Mom wouldn't let me get my license until she got back from Egypt and could let me do more practice driving. That's what she said, but the real reason was so she wouldn't have to worry about me driving while she was gone. So for starters, my only transportation would be my bike. My best friends in Minnetonka, Erica and Sara, were gone for the summer, too, out of cell phone reach. Erica and her parents were spending the summer in England, and Sara and her oboe were off at Interlochen music camp in Michigan where there were strict rules about cell phones. So Mom had cancelled our cell phone contract for the whole summer. No pleading mattered. Her response was, "You earn enough money to buy your own phone and policy this summer, you go right ahead."

✖✖

After pie, I took off on my mountain bike without offering to help with dishes. I rode the bluffs beyond Scout's place.

Scout's house sits near the edge of a rocky cliff overlooking the Blue Earth River. The back of his house is connected, by a huge shop and garage and then a passageway, to the back room of Scout's Last Chance, the bar and grill he owns. The building is as wide as Scout's backyard, so even though the front of the bar and grill opens onto a parking lot, you can't even see the parking lot from Scout's house. The trees come up thick to the sides of the bar and grill, a border around Scout's yard. The woods stretch out from there, and steep trails slope down to the water.

I swooped down a sand hill and tooled around the jumps and logs by the water. It should have been a stunning spot, with the river and hills and woods and all, but it was a junk pit. Wildflowers bloomed purple, yellow, and white, and the trees were a bright early summer green, but garbage littered the beauty, more colorful than the wildflowers. Not just cans and bottles and candy wrappers. A water heater. Broken chairs. A table with two legs. A shoe. A rope. A ripped sweater. A pile of tires. Beer cans. People must have just driven in, dumped their crap, and taken off. I dodged a water softener beside the trail.

After about an hour, a voice drifted down the hill and I stopped, one foot down, to listen. "Sadie! Sadie!" I turned my bike uphill, toward Uncle Scout's voice. "Sadie?" I stood on my pedals and cranked up the steep sandy slope.

"Coming!" I yelled.

"Get your wiry butt up here if you want to watch the show!"

"Here she is," Uncle Thomas bellowed. "Time for the unveiling!"

The whole family—cousins, Grandma, and all—crowded around Uncle Thomas's trailer, which was hooked behind his pickup. I wheeled over to them.

"What are you boys up to this time?" Grandma asked.

"No worries, Mum."

Grandma patted her hair waves and crossed her arms.

Uncle Scout set a case of MGD on the pickup tailgate and he and Thomas each cracked a can. Two in the afternoon, and it was their second case of the day. Mom's brothers are both huge men—they could have auditioned for the part of Hagrid in *Harry Potter*—and they were a little tipsy.

"I'm sorry," Aunt Janie said to my mom and to Aunt Susan.

"Sorry?" Aunt Susan said. "What for?"

Aunt Janie tried to smile, but it didn't work. "It's something Thomas has always wanted," she said, "so when I found one on eBay, I got it for him. He's like a little kid with it."

The trailer door slid open and Uncle Scout fairly screamed, "Holy shit!"

"Jack Landan Hoelschmeier!" Aunt Susan yelled. "There are eight children present and you *watch* your mouth."

"He said *holy shit!*" the kids too young to know better (which meant all the kids except me) whispered, giggling.

"And she called him *Jack,*" I said. "Watch out."

Scout and Thomas came down the ramp, pulling and steadying a full-sized, genuine Civil War cannon.

I don't know what I was expecting to be in the trailer, but certainly not a real live cannon. Well, not *live,* but real.

"You're not going to—" Susan started to say.

"What exactly," Scout said, chucking her on the chin in his most tender teasing manner, "is a cannon for, my dear, if not to *fire?*"

"You sure that's a good idea?" Mom, the liberal of the crowd, looked a little panicky. She hates guns, period. And nobody knows her brothers better than Mom does.

"Settle down, pipsqueak," Scout said.

She glowered at him and he laughed. Scout is the only one in the world who can get away with calling my mother *pipsqueak*. Not even Thomas, the youngest of the three, would dare.

I leaned my mountain bike against the porch and stood beside Mom to watch.

Both Scout and Thomas are Civil War freaks. They dress up like Union soldiers, do reenactments of the war, and shoot authentic black-powder rifles. Thomas is a colonel in the Civil War enactment regiment, for whatever that's worth. Sounds like glorified Boy Scouts to me. Right now they were wearing half of their Civil War uniforms. They hadn't bothered with the official pants, but they had the shirts on, hanging open over their T-shirts and jeans, the jackets on top, and the blue Union hats jammed cock-eyed on their heads.

Scout and Thomas pulled the cannon out to the bluff. They faced it out over the Blue Earth River toward the field beyond, which was bright green with baby corn plants, fresh out of the ground after spring planting.

Scout and Thomas were tipsy enough not to be in perfect control of their senses, and they were finding themselves very funny. Scout lit himself a cigar, offered one to Thomas, who waved it away. They put four cannonballs in a little pile, chuckling to themselves. "Just to look authentic," Uncle Thomas said.

They poured in some gun powder, tamped it down the cannon barrel with a plunger, and loaded one cannon ball from the small stack.

Thomas dabbed at his face with his hanky. All this exertion was making him sweat.

"Do you know what you're doing?" Aunt Janie asked. "That thing did *not* come with instructions."

"Easy, woman. Do you know anyone who knows his way around firearms as well as we do?" Thomas said.

"That's what scares me." Her sigh filled about as much space as Thomas's body. She forced all of us, the kids and Aunt Susan and Mom and Grandma included, to back up about thirty feet behind the cannon as the guys got ready to shoot.

Scout and Thomas were hopping around like giant little boys with firecrackers on the Fourth of July. "We're finally ready!" bellowed Thomas. He squatted by one cannon wheel, well out of the line of fire.

Scout took a big drag on his cigar so the end glowed bright red. He held it high for a ceremonial moment, then brought it down to the cannon's touch-hole. It sparked, he dropped to a crouch, and there was a flash from the touch-hole just like in the movies, and then POP! And the cannon ball popped out of the cannon and blooped into the grass fifteen feet in front of the men. It hadn't even made it into the river.

We all erupted in howls of laughter, Thomas and Scout, too.

"HAhaHa!" Thomas said, standing, holding the shaking mass of flesh between his Union uniform jacket and his rib cage. Then he pulled out his bandana and mopped his face again. "That was obviously not enough powder!"

"Wait," Susan begged. "We all survived this once. Don't you think you should quit while you're ahead?"

Uncle Scout's eyes twinkled. "Ahead? That's not ahead. That was barely going forward. That doesn't even count as firing the thing."

Aunt Susan shrugged.

Uncle Scout actually trotted to the house to get more gunpowder from his gun cabinet. It was like an earthquake of flesh. I swear, the ground shook. I had *never* seen Uncle Scout trot before.

Peapod, Scout's yellow lab, didn't like the cannon. He whined and scratched at the door and dashed inside the second Scout opened it.

Scout came back lugging a three-gallon powder keg like a pirate's treasure.

"Let's see," Scout said. "If that much powder just gave a tiny *bloop*, then we need at least five times that for a hefty shot, don't ya think?"

"At least," Thomas said, turning the keg up to pour some more—a *lot more*—of its contents into the cannon chamber.

Janie gave herself the sign of the cross. Mom saw that and laughed, but together, they backed us up even farther this time.

The men tamped the powder and loaded another cannonball. Susan and Janie put their hands over their ears. "Cover your ears," Janie said, but none of us kids did.

Finally, Scout held his now-stubbier cigar to the touch-hole again. It sparkled just like before, jumped to a full-fledged flash, and I saw flames shooting out the cannon barrel a split second before the air around me cracked in two with a boom that seemed to break my sternum and rupture my eardrums and suck the oxygen right out of the air.

Now I knew why they use the word "deafening." When the boom went away, no other sound came back. Everything was dead, deafened silence in our damaged eardrums as we watched that cannonball hurl skyward, sailing up, up, over the river and over the horizon, arcing out of sight in a southerly direction.

I could see Uncle Scout's mouth moving, but I couldn't hear a word he said. I could see the giant grin on Thomas's face and I could see them start to shake with laughter, but there were no sounds getting through my imploded eardrums. Adam, Thomas and Janie's four-year-old, turned toward me and I could see his face screwed up in an all-out wail, but I couldn't hear it. I picked him up, but he reached for his mom and Janie took him.

I could see the men's laughter subsiding as they looked in the direction the cannonball went and then at each other. I could read Uncle Scout's lips. "Holy shit."

Thomas said something back, and then they turned sheepishly in the direction of their wives.

Susan's face was scarlet. I'd never seen her that color in all the years I've known her, since I was four and the flower girl at their wedding. Janie's face was white. She was still holding one ear, with Adam in her other arm, and staring in the direction where the cannonball had disappeared. Mom stood with her mouth hanging open and shaking with laughter.

An answering BOOM resounded out of the south.

"Holy shit!" I heard Uncle Scout say, and I realized my eardrums were moving again.

We wheeled to look, and over the edge of the world, we could see a plume of gray smoke and debris shooting upward. We stood, open-mouthed, until there was another BOOM and flames shot toward the sky, then black smoke, thick as tar, billowed into a column against the deep blue.

"Oh my stars," Grandma said, holding her chest.

"You'd better get yourselves down there and see what the heck you just blew up," Aunt Susan said.

Janie's face had gone from white to ghostly. Adam on her hip, she grabbed six-year-old Alicia's hand, whirled on her heel, and dragged both kids into the house, slamming the door.

The rest of us stood there gaping. Mom put one hand on my shoulder. "That was loud enough to wake the dead," she said.

"The dead soldiers?" Timmy asked.

"What?" Mom said.

"All the dead soldiers? For Memorial Day?"

"You dork," I said.

"Was s'posed to be a joke," Timmy said.

"It was almost funny." I gave him a soft little punch in the shoulder. He stuck out his tongue at me and ran over to Stevie.

Thomas swiped his face with his hanky and Scout shook his head, as if the big boys were trying to shake off the beer and sober up on the spot. They walked wordlessly to Scout's pickup, hoisted their heavy carcasses up and into it (which lowered the pickup on its springs a good four inches), and took off down the road in the direction of the cannonball landing. The last thing I saw was Thomas pulling out his everlasting blue hanky and dabbing at his ever-sweating face one more time.

Aunt Susan, my mom, and Grandma herded the little kids into the house. I ran for my bike. "Sadie, you be careful," my mom yelled at me as she pulled the screen door shut.

I'd gone about a quarter mile down the blacktop when two police cars blasted past me, sirens wailing, and then a fire truck. Then another.

By the time I got to the corner, the road was filling up with cars and pickups—people coming to see what the explosion was. Rubberneckers, my dad always calls them.

At the corner, I turned toward Norton Roberts' place, nearly a mile from Scout's. Behind his house, a thick pillar of black smoke was billowing up to the sky. I felt a whoosh by my shoulder. A pickup truck's mirror had missed my shoulder by about two inches because the driver was so busy gawking at the fire. I took the ditch.

Another bang sent up a spray of flame and sparks, higher than all the trees on the place. I got to the Roberts' driveway just as the garage sort of burst like fireworks, shooting flames, smoke, and sparks in all directions. That set off a whole series of little explosions. Giant firecrackers for Memorial Day.

A cop guarding the driveway hustled over to me. "You'd better turn around right here, young lady."

"But I'm Scout and Thomas Hoelschmeier's niece. I think they're in trouble."

The cop was bald, and the skin around the edges of his cap looked almost crispy from the heat of the fire. "You bet they're in trouble, little lady. So much trouble, you'd better git yourself home and wait for 'em."

"But—"

"No buts, little lady." He lifted his cap and swiped at his face. Beads of sweat stood on his shiny head. The fire was that hot all the way to the road.

I'm not *a lady,* I wanted to yell at him. *Quit calling me that.* But he looked so crabby that I didn't say anything.

"You git on home."

I just stared at him.

"Git!"

So I got.

TWO

Junk Woods

May 28, continued

I rode as slowly as I could, not toward Scout's. I took the ditches and stayed on the part of the road where I could watch the fire and the black column of smoke over my shoulder. The thick tarry smell hung in the air for almost a mile. Past it, the sky was deep blue, and I rode and rode. When I figured I'd better turn around, I wheeled back and found a path by the river, through the woods, that I thought should lead to Uncle Scout's.

Leaves flanked the trail with bright spring green. I could see the pillar of dark smoke from here but couldn't smell it, so I lifted my nose to breathe it all in like a dog: the sky, the leaves, the wildflowers, the scent of damp earth and new things growing. I cranked around a corner. The trees grew thicker, and I was back in the junk woods. Antifreeze jugs, hubcaps, tires, pieces of a snowmobile, a broken motorcycle helmet, a refrigerator door. At least I was on the right path to Scout's. "Welcome to the junk woods," I said out loud. I rode even slower, watching for glass and nails.

I climbed the hill out of the river bottom and the trees dissolved into a clearing: the edge of a trailer court. This was in town, because LeHillier was inside the Mankato city limits as far as I knew, but the trailers squatted on squares between *dirt* roads. Dust hung in the air and diluted the blue sky into an orangish-brown haze. Garbage was piled near every—*every*—trailer. Junked cars and four-wheeler ATVs sat in yards.

A woman in a saggy, dingy white T-shirt sat on her steps, her bony knees sticking out from cut-offs, a cigarette between her lips and a can of Pabst in her yellowed, bony fingers. A German Shepherd beside her jumped up and barked. She said something to him, cigarette dangling and bobbing on her lips, and he sat instantly in the dirt beside her steps and they both watched me wheel past.

Farther down the dirt road, a pitbull-looking dog lunged to the end of his chain and growled at me. I pedaled faster.

Past the trailer court, I came to Mankato's Waste Management Center: a huge recyclables drop-off facility and sleeping quarters for the local fleet of garbage trucks. In back, a Dumpster cemetery sprawled, a Red Sea of rusty decrepit Dumpsters rolling off their broken wheels in the meadow, daisies springing up among them. Creepy. I'd never thought about where Dumpsters go when they're too busted to be useful. Birds sang, and I could only imagine the rats and mice that figured they'd hit the jackpot for spacious condo living. I pedaled even faster.

But the world got even stranger. First, a semi-truck loomed between the Red Sea and the woods. This parked, deserted semi looked to be in perfect condition, all intact, with bright shiny red paint—except for the fact that vines had grown all over it, covering its sides, swallowing up the hood, the cab, the doors, as if the vines were ravenous, consuming it. As if somebody had driven it all day, parked it, and overnight the vines took over. A Stephen King truck.

Beyond the vine truck, I rode into the trailer home cemetery. Junked trailer homes, one after another, lay like a bunch of dead dinosaurs sprawled through an acre of woods. Except somehow, these homes didn't seem quite dead.

I stopped, my feet on the ground, and surveyed a trailer that had been rolled on its side. It didn't have a floor. Bottoms of the bathtub and sink, rusty pipes like giant curling snakes, coils of the stove, and undersides of drawers and cupboards were still intact. I felt as if I was looking up some giant fat lady's skirt. I wanted to get out of there as fast as I could, but I couldn't stop staring. It was like peering at some intimate disaster where I had no business looking. Or like watching a horror movie when you want to turn it off, but can't peel your eyes off the screen.

I clipped my cleat back into my pedal and turned toward Scout's.

I nearly fell over.

There, sitting on the crossbar of her orange Kona mountain bike, staring at me, was a girl with more hardware on her face than I'd ever seen—an ear studded all the way around in earrings, an eyebrow ring, a nose ring, a lip ring, and shock-white hair sticking up straight around and through her silver cycling helmet. Staring, and not smiling. Her hair made an eerie halo, so I had this panicky feeling that she was a ghost from one of the dead dinosaur trailers. But she was way too tan to be a ghost.

"Oh! Hi," I said. "You scared the crap out of me."

She jerked her head toward the dead mobile homes. "Lovely, isn't it?"

I nodded. "I didn't know it was legal to dump that much junk anywhere and get away with it."

"It's not legal. But it's private property."

I stared.

"You haven't seen nothin' yet. Even grosser deeper in the woods. Guy who owns it is an ass, if you wondered what I thought about him."

"Uh—I didn't really have time to wonder."

The hard line of the girl's jaw loosened and amusement crept up her face. I started to smile at her, but then our eyes locked, a sort of duel to see what who would make the next move. I felt like a preppy goody-two-shoes with my clean, smooth face and brown ponytail.

Finally, her eyes twinkled and she cracked into a grin. "Ride much?"

I shrugged. "As much as I can."

She nodded, taking in my Giant Yukon mountain bike, my legs, my arms. She herself looked rock-hard, from her eyes to her shoulders to her quads and her calves. Even when she was relaxed on her bike, her muscles seemed to bulge. She wore a neon orange tank-top jersey and you could draw a line along the separation of her shoulder, biceps, and triceps. "Race?" she said.

"Huh?" I asked. I couldn't quite imagine where she wanted to race me in this junkyard woods.

"You race your bike?" she asked.

"Oh. No," I said. "I want to." That sounded lame. I shook my head, worked my front brake lever. "Not yet. Keep thinking about it." I looked back up at her. "Guess I'm chicken."

"Just gotta do it anyway. Wanna go for a ride? With me, I mean?"

I shrugged again. Scout and Thomas wouldn't be back for quite a while. The aunts wouldn't be any happier than they were when I left. A longer ride couldn't hurt. "Sure."

And so I followed her. Her thighs were so cut that from the back, you could see the quads bulging above her knee.

The hardware girl was strong. And fast.

Out of the woods, down the hill, past Scout's Last Chance, across Highway 60, I tailed her. Back into the woods on the other side of the highway. "Been down here?" she asked.

"No."

"This is the other river. Minnesota. The one back where we just were is the Blue Earth River. They merge in town. That's why they call Mankato the 'Bend of the River.' Did you know that?"

I was breathing so hard from keeping up, all I could answer was, "No."

"You're new here."

"Yeah."

"Thought so. I thought I knew all the mountain bikers in town."

She rode down a rutty, bumpy, rocky dirt road. The descent was so sharp I had to feather my back brake constantly. She looked over her shoulder to check on me from time to time. We went under a railroad trestle where the rocks were as big as bread loaves. It was like riding down a stairway. If I were alone, I'd have gotten off and walked down the bumps, but I couldn't do that with her there. I couldn't be chicken, but I was sweating bullets. This was scary. I tried to watch where she put her wheel and follow the same line.

It worked most of the way; then, at the bottom, there was a sharp turn into soft sandy dirt, and I oversteered and felt myself flying over the handlebars. The dirt came flying at me, and smack, I was on my back in the weeds. "Oof." A rock dug into my back, too, but just by my shoulder blade. Nothing vital.

The hardware girl's brakes squeaked. "You okay?" She clicked one foot out of her clip-in pedal and set it on the ground to look back at me.

"Yeah, fine." I jumped up, brushed off my butt. "Just stupid."

She eyed me. "Not stupid. That's a tricky descent. You're good." She wheeled back to me and stuck out her hand. "I'm Allison Baker. Allie."

"Sadie Lester."

"Sadie." Her handshake was so firm it was almost scary. Like a man's. "Sadie. I never knew anybody named Sadie." She clipped back into her pedals. "Except my cousin's Doberman. Let's go, Sadie Lester."

We were off. The road disintegrated to four-wheeler tracks that followed the Minnesota River. It was less technical than the downhill we just rode, but tricky and the sand was powdery in places. The river flowed wide and calm and murky. We rode and rode until we ran out of trail.

Then we pedaled up a steep grassy hill, jounced over some railroad tracks, and hit the shoulder of a paved road. I had never ridden harder in my whole life.

When we stopped, I said, "I better get back."

"Where do you live?" she asked.

"Behind Scout's Last Chance."

Her eyebrow ring went up, in a question she didn't say out loud.

"Scout's my uncle. I'm staying for the summer. I—just got here. Today."

She nodded. "Let's ride again, Sadie Lester. See ya around."

"Okay—" I started to ask for a phone number or something, but she was gone, pedaling off in the direction away from Scout's.

When I tooled into the driveway, the cannon was put away in its trailer. Mom and Thomas and Scout were standing in the yard, not with happy faces.

"Where have you been?" Mom's face was pinched with anger and worry.

"Riding. Why?"

"You've been gone almost three hours! When Scout and Tom got back, they said they never saw you. And there are lots of freaks out on the road today. I was scared silly. Besides, I need to get going. My plane leaves at five in the morning, you know."

"If you're so worried about me, why are you leaving me for the summer?" That wasn't fair, but I couldn't resist. "I'm fine, Mom. I met a girl out riding, and she showed me a bunch of trails."

I could tell she was torn between being glad I'd met a friend already and being mad. So she said, "Good thing for your sake we have plenty of other stuff to worry about."

"What?"

Scout explained. The cannon ball had put a hole clear through the back wall of the Roberts' garage. But if that wasn't enough, the cannonball landed squarely on Norton

Roberts' four-month-old Audi; the gas tank exploded, and the thing went up like a bomb. That was the first boom we'd heard. Worse yet, parked right beside the impeccable car was Norton's irreplaceable, restored classic 1974 Norton motorcycle. Norton's Norton. His pride and joy. While the garage was burning down, of course the Norton's gas tank blew up in the flames, too. Not good, any way you look at it. Everyone expects a few minor explosions on the Fourth of July. But Memorial Day? Leave it to Uncle Scout and Uncle Thomas.

There would be a hearing on Wednesday.

When we were alone, I said, "Mom, you gonna leave Timmy and me with *them* for the summer? Isn't that negligence or something?"

"Hush," she said, and I thought she might cry, so I hushed.

She walked Timmy and me to the edge of the woods, promised she'd call us at least once a week from Egypt. For our sake, she was trying not to act too excited about Egypt. Or too worried about leaving us. I couldn't muster up any excitement for her.

"Bye, Mom. Have fun. Yeah, love you, too," was all I could give her with my hug. Then her Subaru disappeared around Scout's bar and grill and turned up Highway 60.

THREE

CCC

May 28, continued

Timmy moved into Stevie's bedroom with glee. Stevie is nine, a year older than Timmy, so they were thrilled to death about the summer arrangements.

I wasn't.

After Thomas and Janie and kids left, Aunt Susan turned to me. "You have a couple choices. You can move in with Megan." Megan is only seven, not even half as old as me. "Or you can move into my sewing room. It's sort of a mess, but you'd have privacy. I never have time to sew in the summer, so I don't use the room. It's up to you."

I picked privacy, and Megan started to wail.

"Look, Megan," I said. "I'll see you every day anyway. But I like to read and stay up late, and it would be a pain to have me banging around in your room every single day. And you wouldn't like my music."

"Yes I would! I want to listen to your music."

I sighed. "You can come listen to music with me sometimes. And"—I was afraid I'd regret this part—"and we can do other stuff together, maybe even go on bike rides."

Her waterworks turned off instantly. *Little manipulator.*

The sewing room was really a closet in the basement. It used to be the root cellar a hundred years ago, but Scout put cinder blocks and cedar paneling down there to make a room for Susan. Susan had crafty stuff all over the house. Timmy said the house was "crowdy" with stuff Susan had made, and he was right. All the overflow "crowdy" stuff had been crammed into my bedroom closet. Shelves and shelves of cloth and styrofoam balls and yarn and fake wheat and silk flowers and stuff. Just great. I was going to live in Hobby Lobby. At least it smelled like cedar.

"Nice," I said.

"It's not *nice*," she said. "And it's a disaster, but it is *private*."

"Thanks," I said.

This is your bed," she said, pulling out the fold-out couch and handing me sheets and one blanket. I'd brought my own pillow. "You can rearrange anything you like. Just please don't throw anything out. I might want it sometime."

I nodded, thinking that in a million years she couldn't use all the crap in the room. But I just nodded like I agreed.

A reading lamp was perched on a tiny table at the end of the couch-bed, and the magazines on the table were this month's. She'd lied about not using this room. This was her only hideout, away from the rest of the household, and she was giving it to me.

"I'm sorry," I said.

"For what?"

"Taking your room. I could stay with Megan. Really. I just thought—"

"No," she interrupted me. "A sixteen-year-old has no place sharing a room with a seven-year-old. Let me feel good about one thing, just one thing, this summer, okay?"

"Thanks." I hugged her 'cause I thought I should, but her face sagged, and I could tell she was already sorry she had two extra bodies in her house for the summer.

I vacuumed and piled up some stuff that was on the floor. I even wiped down the walls with a rag because I discovered that they smell more like cedar if you rub them. I wondered if I could get high, smelling it. When the bed was folded open, I had two feet on each side of the room to move around. I figured I'd fold the bed up during the day. It was a closet, and there were no windows. At least I wouldn't have to get out of bed if a tornado blasted through town. A bit of privacy was worth a ton of claustrophobia. I made a sign and put it on the door:

"Cedar Claustrophobia Central. Please knock before entering. Thanks. Signed, Sadie, Management, C.C.C."

"Very funny," Aunt Susan said.

FOUR

Jail

May 30

Wednesday, the big boys, Janie, and Susan went to court. I had to babysit everybody. It was mayhem, but we played croquet and I made frozen pizza for lunch. It wasn't as bad as it could have been.

It got worse when the adults got home. They were stone quiet.

Janie and Thomas didn't even say hi. They just picked up their kids, got in Thomas's truck, and took off. Scout's and Susan's faces were so long I didn't dare ask what happened. But Scout told me I could come in his study while he called Mom to give her the news.

"No jury trial," he said. "Just a judge's sentence. Reckless endangerment. Illegal discharge of firearms within city limits. Public drunkenness. Operating a motor vehicle under the influence...yeah...willful and careless destruction of property. Norton Roberts is one pissed-off dude. He's ruthless, and his lawyer is a shark—the lawyer went on a rant. He said, 'Nothing, *nothing* can restore Norton's Norton.' So guess what?"

I couldn't hear Mom's answer.

"Nope. Goin' to jail."

I sucked in my breath. I could almost hear Mom doing the same. "Tomorrow morning. Can't believe it."

FIVE

The Blue Ox

May 31

So the next morning, the big boys went to jail. Aunt Susan quit smiling entirely, and Timmy and I were stuck for the whole long summer in a house with a new total of six kids and one depressed aunt.

My first order of business was to get a job.

I asked Marley, Scout's cook and manager, if I could work at Scout's Last Chance, but they serve alcohol—that's what a bar and grill *is*—so they couldn't legally hire a sixteen-year-old, even to bus tables or wash dishes. Marley said, "Scout might hire you and just pay you cash, but I don't feel okay doing that. I don't want to get him in any more trouble than he already is."

I wanted to work somewhere I could get tips. So I rode my bike across town to fill out an application at the Blue Ox, a greasy-spoon diner/truck stop/gas station that specialized in Paul-Bunyan-sized twenty-four-ounce steaks. A twelve-foot Babe the Blue Ox stood guard near the rustic hitching post between the parking lot and the door. I leaned my bike against Babe's front leg and reached up and touched his nose for luck before I went in.

Barb, one of the owners, interviewed me. She could have been my grandma's twin, but Barb was hard around the edges where Grandma was soft as cotton (except for the calluses where life had rubbed against too much hard work and too many people she loved who had died). Barb's hard edges made me think everything that had rubbed against her life had hurt. Her voice sounded deep and thick from cigarette smoke.

I got the job. I had to wear a uniform: a bandana somewhere on my body (she gave me one red and one blue), a checkered shirt (she gave me one blue and one red), and jeans. I was supposed to start the next day for the breakfast shift. I had to be there at five o'clock a.m. for a half hour of training. Usually breakfast shift started at five thirty, but not on my first day.

SIX

And a Wet Dog

June 1

It wasn't really light enough to see, riding my bike across town, so I swiped a flashlight from the junk drawer. But there wasn't much traffic to worry about.

I bussed tables, learned the shorthand for the kitchen, and only spilled coffee on one table.

The place sported red-checkered tablecloths. It was the first time in my life I felt like I blended in with the furniture. And it was the first time in my life I watched people eat mammoth steaks for *breakfast*. I couldn't imagine. I watched fat men chew steak at six thirty a.m., and I debated becoming a vegetarian right then and there.

✖✖

When I got home at eleven fifteen that morning, all the little kids were swarming around the house.

"How was it?" Susan asked without looking up.

"Okay," I said.

Susan was wearing a faded green T-shirt that read *Walk for Hope*. Stooped over the sink, she reminded me of a hopeless stalk of wilted celery. She brushed hair out of her face with the back of her dishpan hand and asked, "Will you take Peapod for a walk? Scout always walks him in the morning. I don't have time."

I changed my clothes.

When I came back upstairs, Megan was waiting to pounce on me. "Can I go? Can I go?"

"Okay," I said. "Peapod, come on!"

"Girls," Aunt Susan said, "don't go *anywhere* near that trailer court. Hear?"

Peapod bounced around, thrilled to death. Anybody who says dogs don't smile is insane. He bounced his sleek golden self high enough to slurp my cheek and tore circles around us, waiting to find out which direction we were going.

"Let's go to the river," Megan said.

So we headed into the woods, toward the trails above the river. Peapod bounced ahead, out of sight, and then came bounding back to check on us.

The woods was full of birds and squirrels. I saw lady-slippers and jack-in-the pulpits. And I love the bright green of early summer. I breathed it in, like I always do, and was glad not to smell smoke this time. I couldn't wait to get out on my bike. We came around a bend in the trail, and once again, the litter seemed to spring from the ground thicker than the wildflowers. Everywhere. Whiskey bottles, newspapers, broken plates, a smashed TV, a water heater, beer cases, carpeting, a swivel chair, and couch cushions. I could have stepped on junk like stepping-stones, all through the woods, if I'd concentrated on it. "The junk woods," I said out loud.

"Yup," Megan said. "Sometimes we find treasures."

"I bet."

We reached the steep slope down to the river. The water sparkled in the sun.

"Want to swim?" I asked Peapod.

He looked at me, ears cocked, and wagged.

"Want to go swim?" I said again.

He jumped straight in the air and took off down the rest of the steep path so fast I think his feet touched the ground four times in fifty feet. He disappeared around a corner, and we heard him splash into the water.

When Megan and I got down to the riverbank, Peapod grinned up at us over the rippling surface of the water and splashed some more. He fished in the shallows, stalking minnows or bullheads and pouncing on them, paws down, nose up. He didn't catch anything, but Megan said, "He caught a crawdad once. He's been a fisherdog ever since."

Megan took my hand and we walked along the trail by the river. Peapod followed us in the water, pouncing at regular intervals. We stepped around bottles, a fender, chunks of Plexiglass, tires, and a ragged T-shirt among the weeds and scrubby fir trees. Another curve, and dead in front of us was a big tagboard sign, hand-written and nailed to a tree:

Whoever took my chain saw you better bring it back or I will find you and fuck you up Steve Olsen 386-0014

I stopped and stared at the thing. The magic-marker letters were crooked, and ran downhill on each line. And who with half a brain would write a note like that and sign his name? And leave a phone number?

"What does it say?" Megan asked. She started to read aloud, "Who-ever took my—what's that?"

"Chain saw," I said. "Let's go home."

"Wait! I want to read it."

She finished aloud. "F—uck. Fuck!? It says *fuck* on a sign? That's bad, bad word, Mommy says."

"It's a bad sign, Megan," I said. "It gives me the creeps. Let's get out of here. Peapod, come on."

Peapod came bounding and shook dirty river water all over us.

"Ick!" Megan squealed. "Stop it, stupid Peapod!"

We followed Peapod uphill. Each wag of his tail sent arcs of dirty water at us. Again, he paused every now and then to check that we were right behind him, as well as to shake.

When we reached Scout's, Megan said, "Daddy sprays him off when he's been in the river." So we hosed him down and toweled him off with shop rags from the garage. Peapod gave me happy slurps through the whole process.

"He misses Dad," Megan said. "But he likes you lots."

I nodded. If I was going to be Peapod's substitute favorite human while Scout was in jail, that was okay with me.

We didn't tell Aunt Susan about the chain-saw sign.

SEVEN

AllieCat

June 1, continued

I helped Aunt Susan feed the kids peanut butter sandwiches and peaches for lunch, clear the table, and stack the dishwasher. Then I said, "I'm going to go for a ride, okay?"

She sighed. A big sigh. "I suppose."

I ran to my CCC closet to get ready before she could change her mind.

I was wheeling my Giant out the garage door when Allie came sailing around the corner of the Last Chance and skidded to a stop six inches from my front tire.

"Good timing," she said. "I was just wondering if you wanted to ride. I cruised by here once and didn't see anybody."

"Man, am I glad to see you. I gotta get out of there."

"I hear ya."

"You gotta give me your phone number, so we can plan this instead of just wondering."

She jerked her head over her shoulder. "Let's go this way. I want to show you Mount Kato." And she took off.

I stared at her back, and barely had time to wonder why she didn't answer about her phone number as I threw my leg over my bike, clipped in, and followed.

Allie stood in her pedals and looked back at me. "So why are you here, Sadie Lester?" She grinned. "I mean, why are you staying at your uncle's place?"

"My mom's gone for the summer. So she sorta dumped me and my brother with Uncle Scout."

"Isn't he in jail? That's what I heard."

I felt like scum of the earth having to answer, "Yeah."

"'S'okay," she said. "I've known people in jail."

"You have?"

"Let's go," she said. And turned up the pace so all I could do was pedal.

We followed the road for a ways, then Allie ducked onto a doubletrack trail in the ditch where four-wheelers had worn the grass down to the dirt. At the intersection, we hopped on the paved bike trail for about two miles to Mount Kato.

"This is where they have races," she said. "Mountain bike races. It's a ski hill all winter, but it's full of bike trails in the back. You gotta get a pass. Then we can ride those trails. Get you ready for the race."

"Race?"

"Fourth of July. You're doing it. I already told Mike to sign you up."

"Mike?"

"The bike shop owner. A-1 Bike. He's putting the race on."

"When were you gonna tell me that you signed me up?"

"I just did." Allie grinned. "It's only twenty bucks. You can swing that, can't you? You said you were chicken, so I thought I'd give you a little push. Come on!" And she was off again, cranking uphill this time, away from the mountain biking and ski hill. And I was chasing her wheel again.

We left a gravel road and followed more doubletrack trail through woods. Allie guided her tires down a short, steep slope into a stream, between the rocks and through the water. I missed following her line by about an inch and hit a minor boulder instead of smooth creekbed. My rear tire came up and the water rushed at me. After the first shock, the water felt good.

She stopped to wait for me. "Wish I had a camera."

I sat up, water swirling around my rear end and my ankles, and pushed to my feet. "How come you *always* land on your feet—on your wheels?"

"Not always."

"I don't believe you." I stepped out of the creek. Water ran from my shorts.

"Look." Allie set her bike down and came over to me. "Look. And look." She pointed to scars on her legs and elbows and one shoulder, healed and embedded in her deep tan. I hadn't noticed. "Times I didn't land on my wheels.

This is not a sport for beauty queens." She lifted the edge of her bike short to remind me of our funny bikers' tan lines.

"But now, you always land rubber-side down," I said. "You're like an alley cat."

She laughed. "You're not the first person to call me that. Some of the guys that race call me AllieCat."

"And here I thought I was being so creative." I rescued my bike and squeezed more water out of the rear end of my shorts.

"Too bad," she said. "They beat ya to it. And Sadie?"

"Yeah?"

"The only people who aren't chicken are a little stupid. You just gotta ride anyway. Ride *through* the chicken, you might say. Come on."

Allie and I rode out of the woods, me still squishy-wet, over gravel roads and hills and bridges. I dried some from the heat and sun, but mostly I got too sweaty to notice. We got chased by two farm dogs and a crazed-looking old woman under a yellow-brimmed hat who gunned her John Deere garden tractor in our direction. "You nincompoops!" she screamed. "You're gonna scare my goats!" We rode away as fast as we could.

At the top of the next hill, we spun slowly to catch our breath. "You *nincompoops!*" Allie said, laughing. "You think she'd have mowed us down if she caught us?"

From here, we could see some of Mankato. "Look," Allie said. "There's Father Malcolm's church."

"What?"

She slowed, almost to a stop. "The church by the courthouse. See it?"

"Not really. I can see three churches. Who's Father Malcolm?"

"Just a priest I know. The bronzy-colored steeple. See?"

"Yeah."

"You surprised I know a priest?"

"Not really. Why would I be?"

She was already picking up speed on a long gravel descent, and she shot out of hearing range.

✖✖

We pulled into the Last Chance parking lot after three hours of riding. "Can you ride tomorrow?" Allie asked.

"Yeah. I work until eleven thirty."

"I work 'til noon."

"Where do you work?"

"A bakery. Meet ya at one o'clock in front of the Last Chance." And she was gone.

My legs were so tired they shook while I leaned against the wall in the shower.

EIGHT
Stitches

June 2

The next day at 12:59, Allie sailed up to the Last Chance steps and skidded sideways to a stop in the gravel.

Peapod rose from his cool spot in the shade and wagged over to her without barking. Allie let him sniff her hand. "You smell my dog, don't you?"

"What kind of dog you got?" I asked.

"Mutt. German shepherd, mostly." She rubbed behind Peapod's ears. "What's this guy's name?" she asked.

"Peapod."

"Peapod! What kind of name is that for a big bruiser Lab like you?" she asked him. She got off her bike, sat on the step, and rubbed him until he spilled over on his back for her to rub his tummy. "Why'd Scout name him Peapod?"

"When he was a puppy," I explained, "he looked like a golden peapod when he slept, Scout said. It stuck."

Peapod licked her hand. He would have purred if a dog could purr. Finally I said, "Should we go?"

"Okay." Allie took Peapod's face in both hands, looked him in the eyes and said, "Peapod, you're a good hound. I wonder what you and Siren would think of each other."

"Siren? Your dog is Siren?"

"Yeah, he howls like one."

I laughed.

"Plus, he lets me know when trouble's coming."

"Trouble?"

"Yup." She shrugged and grabbed her bike. "Let's ride."

I followed her rear wheel, trying to imagine what kind of trouble would chase her.

✖✖

Two hours later, covered with sweat and dust—the mixture turning to mud on our arms and legs and faces—we climbed toward the top of the highest hill in the county, according to Allie. I was standing in my lowest gear, creeping pedal over pedal. If I went any slower, I'd fall over.

"They call this 'Embolism Hill,'" she said.

I couldn't breathe enough to say anything in return.

We were close to the top, maybe only a hundred meters from the crest, when my back tire spun out. We were going up at such an angle, and the gravel was so loose, my tread wouldn't catch and I thought I'd go over but I stayed up. "Allie!" I said in gasps, "I'm dyin' here."

"No you're not. You can do this. You just think you're dyin'. Get more weight over the back tire. Center yourself. Breathe. You can do this. Remember..." She was panting, too.

Thank Christ, at least it was hard work for her. My chest was cracking open and my legs were jelly. If this was easy for her, I might have wanted to stab her if I could have, but I couldn't even breathe, much less wield a weapon.

"Remember, if it doesn't kill you, it makes you stronger. Somebody said that." Sadie didn't turn to look at me. She kept her head down, pumping her bike forward. "Ride through the chicken."

"This...is gonna...kill me," I huffed.

"No it's not... It's makin'...you strong. Shut up..." she panted, "...and ride."

And she cranked her bike side to side and rode away from me to the crest of the hill.

A long half minute later, I made it to the top. We spun a quarter mile, letting our legs recover, and then we unclipped, flung ourselves into the grass in the shade of some birch trees, and sat overlooking the Le Sueur River and its valley, sucking on our water bottles and glad for cool grass and shade. We flopped back into the grass and stared through the leaves at the sky, feeling our tired muscles relax and sink toward the center of the earth. The clouds were wisps, free, light on the wind like wild horse tails.

"So, why are you staying with your uncle this summer?" Allie asked.

"My parents are in Egypt."

"Egypt?" She sat up to look at me.

"Yup. Dad's an anthropology professor. An Egyptologist. At the University of Minnesota. He's doing research on Nefertiti."

"Nefer—who?"

I slapped a mosquito. "Nefertiti. Wife of Akhenaten, a pharaoh of Egypt." I looked at her for signs of recognition. She'd obviously never heard of Nefertiti, but she was still listening, so I went on. "My dad has this theory that Akhenaten might have really been Moses in the Bible because he promoted monotheism—belief in one god—in Egypt and then disappeared. They never found his grave. But then they think they found Nefertiti, his wife, so it might blow his theory out of the water." I shrugged. "Who knows." I quit talking. Nothing worse than the kid of a researcher who thinks she knows something.

Allie flopped back in the grass. "Wow. A professor's kid—you're rich and all that. The perfect life."

"Not quite. It's not like that."

"Then how is it?" She half sat, resting on her elbows, staring at me.

I sat up. "My parents are divorced...and Dad had a girlfriend but they broke up, so he invited Mom to come do research with him this summer. So they're both in Egypt."

"Your mom a professor, too?"

"No, she teaches high school history."

"Perfect life, like I said. You have no clue how good you have it," Allie said.

"I don't know how they're getting along over there. They won't talk about that on the phone," I said. "Not perfect."

Allie lay back, pulled a long stem of foxtail grass, and stuck it between her teeth. "Huh. Half the world's divorced. Big deal. You think your dad would want you hanging out with a convict's daughter?"

"A—what did you say?"

"My dad's in prison," she said into the green and blue and white above us, avoiding my eyes.

I absorbed that for a second. "Wh—Where?"

"Stillwater."

"Prison? What for?"

"Breaking the law," she said. "What else?"

I frowned at her. "Yeah, and Scout's in jail for breaking a bunch of laws." I remembered her shrugging that off, saying she knew people who had been in jail. I stared at her, trying to let all this soak in.

She stared back. "You really think that's the same thing?"

"I don't know. You haven't told me what your dad did."

"Whatever." She snorted. She lifted one leg in the air, then the other, wiping salty grime from her shins. Then she propped one ankle on her knee and ran her fingers up the inside of her right calf muscle. "Look," she said. "This is where I sewed myself up."

"You what?"

"Sewed it up myself. Went over the handlebars in a race. Chainring landed here. Ripped it wide open. White fat comin' out the cut. Blood everywhere. Grease, too. When I got home, nobody was around to take me to the doctor, and we don't have health insurance, so Mom probably wouldn't have taken me anyway. So I sewed it up. Poured alcohol in 'til most of the grease came out, then I sewed it up."

I felt my mouth hanging open. She grinned at me. "I finished the race first, though," she said, "bleeding all over the place. I won, too."

The scar was thick and white, bordered with white dots from the needle holes.

"Hurt like hell," she said. "Not sure I could do it again, if you want to know."

"What did you sew it with?"

"A big curved needle and fine fishing line."

I shook my head. I couldn't think of what to say, and I couldn't help looking at all the holes in her ear and her face, too.

She saw what I was thinking. "I know. I'm full of holes. You can tell your dad the professor that you have a holy friend, daughter of a convict."

"Yeah, great," I said. "I'll do that."

She jumped up, grabbed her bike. "Let's go."

That was all the talking we did that day.

NINE

Aunt Susan's Nephew

June 6

A few days later when I got back from the Blue Ox, Aunt Susan was frying bacon for BLTs. "Sadie, will you make toast, please? And slice tomatoes, too?"

I nodded, washed my hands, and started toasting.

Aunt Susan pulled her hand back from the splattering grease. "Ouch. Oh, Sadie. Guess what. One more body to cram into the house." In her yellowed tank top and stringy hair that needed a wash, she looked more like wilted celery than ever, if that were possible.

"Who? Why? You're already overcrowded, aren't you?"

"Your cousin Joseph is coming to stay here, too."

"My cousin? I don't have a cousin Joseph. Do I?"

"Not really. *My* sister's son. Joe is the brother of the kid who died last year. Remember when Scout and I flew to Arizona for a funeral? And dropped the kids off at your place? That kid's twin brother. My sister said he needs to get away for a while."

"How old?" I asked, dropping more bread into the four-slice toaster. "And what happened?—I mean, how did he die?"

"Seventeen. Horrible accident."

I waited for more details, but she sealed her lips and shook her head. Obviously an off-limits topic.

"*Seventeen*? Great. S'pose I have to give up CCC."

Aunt Susan threw me a look over her shoulder and sighed. "I think we'll put a cot in Scout's study. Joe'll be here next week."

I spread mayo on toast. "Why'd you say yes?"

"'Cause I couldn't say no. It's not *all my fault* I'm running a homeless shelter here."

I glared at her back.

She swished three tomatoes under a stream of cold water and handed them to me. "If I remember right, Joe's into biking, too."

"Great. Just great." There would be no escape, even on my bike. The tomatoes spewed bloody juice under my serrated knife.

After lunch, I went into Scout's study and called Mom. "Did you hear about Joe?" I asked.

"Joe?"

"Susan's nephew. This kid's twin brother died, I guess?"

"Oh. Right. I remember. What about him?"

"He's coming to stay, too."

"What? Isn't it going to be *really* crowded in that house? Has Susan lost her mind?"

"It's way too crowded now. And yeah, I'm pretty sure she has. She's sort of wilting away."

"I hope Susan knows what she's doing. Family's good. Too much family isn't."

"Remember, Mom, it was *Scout* who said okay to Timmy and me coming for the summer."

"I know. Are you trying to make me feel guilty?"

"Maybe. Is it working?"

"Stop, okay? I miss you a whole bunch. But it's wonderful to be here."

"You're *thriving*?"

She laughed. "I guess so."

"Think you and Dad will get back together?"

"What's this you mentioned about a mountain bike race?" she asked.

"Way to change the subject, Mom."

"I don't want to talk about Dad right now. We have always worked together well, but I can't imagine we could still be married, Sadie. Don't get your hopes up, please."

I was quiet.

"Okay, Sadie?"

"I'll try. Hey, Mom, do we have health insurance?"

"Of course we have health insurance. Both Dad and I have you on our plans. I gave the insurance cards to Susan. Since when did you start worrying about health insurance?"

"I just wondered, is all."

"What are you doing on your bike, young lady? Why are you asking me this?"

"Something Allie said. She sewed up her own leg 'cause she didn't have insurance, is all."

"Who exactly is this Allie girl?"

"She's cool. She's my friend. The one I met during the cannon ball fire."

"Sadie—"

"I have to go," I interrupted her. No harm in her feeling a *tiny* bit of worry. "I'm meeting Allie in a couple minutes. Have fun digging. Think of us here in the mosquito-infested river valley."

"Very funny. I love you," she said. "Sadie?"

"Hmm?"

"Be careful."

"I love you, too. See ya, Mom."

TEN

Scout

June 8

That Friday, I walked in the door and Aunt Susan was smiling for the first time all summer. "Scout's coming home," she said.

Scout's and Thomas's lawyers appealed their sentences, and had to agree to a bigger fine, but they argued that Norton would get his money faster if the big boys worked rather than sat in jail. Scout would be home on Monday.

I had to ask for a day off from work so I could babysit while Aunt Susan picked him up.

June 11

Scout stepped out of the minivan and the kids mobbed him. He moved across the yard like a giant walking tree, kids hanging off his branches. Peapod leapt in circles around him for five solid minutes. Aunt Susan didn't look so wilted.

Scout grilled burgers and made homemade ice cream. I think he'd lost a little weight in jail, but if the way he ate that day was any indication, he was bent on gaining it back as fast as possible.

ELEVEN

Rednecks and Allie and Me

June 14

Thursday, when I was making change at the cash register for a couple who had eaten twenty-four dollars' worth of steak and given me a fifty-cent tip, a rusty, red-faded-almost-to-orange Grand Am with out-of-state plates pulled up to the Blue Ox's gas pumps.

The first thing that caught my attention was the bike. A mountain bike, a blue Gary Fisher, was strapped in the car-top rack. Full of mud, that mountain bike got *used*. An aluminum ladder with a red warning flag tied on the end hung out of the trunk, a shock of black hair hung over one eyebrow on the driver, and a cigarette hung from the driver's lips.

None of the bikers I knew smoked. Preserve the lungs for long rides. Have reverence for clean air, and all that. This biker smoked. Maybe the bike was just alternative transportation in case the decrepit car gave out. He unfolded himself from the driver's seat, leaned against the car door, and savored a last drag on his cigarette before throwing it out of range of the gas pump.

The cheap-tipper-steak-eaters marked the last of the breakfast rush. The nine o'clock oldster coffee klatch had two full pots on their table, and they could help themselves while they played pinochle. So this dark-haired stranger got all of my attention. I knew he couldn't see me past the red-checkered curtains on the tinted front window. I was safe, gaping at him.

Barb was arranging muffins and cinnamon rolls in the pastry case. She whistled. "Child," she said, "I know you think that one looks good, but to me, he looks good for nothin' but trouble."

I tried to think of something smart to say, but I couldn't. That boy was the sexiest thing I'd ever seen on two legs, off the movie screen. And what would Barb know? She had to be sixty years old.

"Why is it," she asked, "that the good girls always go for the scoundrels?" She humphed back toward the kitchen.

"Is that what you did?" I asked in the direction of her back, not taking my eyes off my customer outside. Good customer service and all.

"What did I do?"

"Were you the good girl who went for a scoundrel?"

"Ha! No, not me."

I turned my head away from the boy outside to look at her.

Barb stopped in the doorway and grinned at me. "I wasn't a good girl." She disappeared behind the swinging door.

I'm afraid my mouth was still hanging open in Barb's direction when *he* came in to pay. They were renovating the gas station area of the truck stop, so everybody who didn't pay at the pump had to pay at the restaurant cash register. He handed me two twenties, and I shook when I counted back his change.

He winked at me. He *winked.* But he didn't say anything. Not a word.

I said, "Thank you, have a nice day" in a croaky version of proper customer service. I smacked myself on both sides of the head as he folded himself back into his car, lit another cigarette, and disappeared up Highway 22.

✖✖

Late in the day, Allie and I rode through the woods like always, then out a gravel road by Lake Crystal and didn't turn back for three hours. When we finally did, Allie said, "We're gonna need to book it to get home before dark now."

We circled back, and finally, we turned onto County Road 68. The traffic was heavy here this evening and we still had several miles to go.

"Glass!" Allie yelled, and swerved toward the ditch. Glass, both red and clear, was strewn across the pavement and shoulder. Somebody had crashed here by the intersection. Behind her, I rolled into the ditch to avoid the mess, but Allie hadn't swerved in time. Twenty feet down the road, her back tire deflated with a *phooph*.

"Shoot."

I slowed to a stop. We both glanced toward the horizon, where earth and sky met, calculating the time until dark. The bottom of the sun was already touching the rim of the world, a giant orange drop ready to be squeezed over the edge by darkness. Probably only forty-five minutes to an hour of light left.

She hopped off the bike, opened her brakes, yanked open the quick-release lever, and slid her rear wheel out of the chain and off the bike. She pried the tire from the wheel, pulled out the punctured inner tube, and ran her thumb around the inside of the tire. Sure enough, her thumb struck a chunk of glass wedged into the rubber between the nubs of tread.

She yanked back her hand. A bright bead of blood rode her thumb. She sucked it clean, and more carefully, she touched the spot again. From the outside of the tire, she pulled a quarter-inch shard of glass and tossed it into the weeds. She checked the rest of the tire, and blew up the inner tube with her mouth to make sure there was only one hole.

She surveyed the ditch and pointed to the remains of a magazine. "Hand me that, will you? That'll work."

I handed it to her. She ripped off a square of glossy paper and placed it inside the tire as a "boot"—to protect the inner tube in case the punctured tire rubber had sharp edges. She pulled a spare inner tube from her jersey pocket and blew into it, inflating it to soft-sausage consistency, then laid it inside the tire, forced the tire back into the metal rim with her thumbs, and pumped it all the way up. Her arm muscles flexed like supple rope.

Finally, she stuffed the limp, punctured tube into her jersey pocket. Mountain bikers always looked like pocket gophers with the pockets on the wrong side, packed full.

Allie glanced at the sky. "We gotta make tracks," she said as she slid her wheel back onto her bike frame.

When the sun sits like a bubble on the horizon, it reminds me of cohesion in chemistry, how one drop of water will stick to a glass when it seems like it shouldn't, how you can get a rounded top on a glass of water (called a meniscus—don't ask me why I remember that, but I do). It's as if the sun is sticking to the sky when it shouldn't, and it tricks your eyes—the sun has really sunk below the horizon, but your eyes hang onto it. Then you look away, and when you look back, the sun has slipped over the edge in one fast *bloop*. Gone.

The sun had slipped away while Allie was changing her tire, and we were riding against time to get back before dark. Neither of us had brought lights.

Allie rode hard, ahead of me, for about forty minutes. I was dripping with sweat, my chest sounded like a locomotive, and dusk was settling in around us.

Allie turned the corner toward Minneopa Cemetery, a steep little eighth-of-a-mile climb. After the descent on the other side, we would only be about two miles from LeHillier.

We stood into the hill, rocking our bikes side to side to get the most forward, uphill thrust for each pedal stroke. Allie is a beautiful climber, smooth as silk, and if you didn't know better you'd think it was easy for her. But it's hard as heck. She just knows how to mask her pain. I caught her rhythm, followed her up, breathing heavier and heavier but watching her smooth, constant pedal cadence. She was so much stronger than me that I was getting a little farther behind, the farther up the hill we went.

Then, behind us, we could hear the roar of glass-pack exhaust on a big vehicle. Sounded like an oversized pickup. Automatically, we both swerved right, off the pavement onto the shoulder to be out of the way, to give him extra room. The truck roared closer. I could see Allie's head go up. She didn't want to turn her head and lose her rhythm, but she rode closer to the outside edge of the shoulder. The glass packs got louder, closer, and suddenly the noise was *too* close. I threw a look behind me in time to see a midnight blue pickup, American flags flapping above each door, bearing down at us, two wheels on the shoulder, spitting gravel, headed straight toward us.

"Hit the ditch!" I screamed, and swerved completely off the road, careening over the edge of the shoulder. My front wheel caught on a rock, sending me catapulting over the handlebars and slamming against the far side of the ditch.

The wind was knocked out of me and the truck roared by, but I could see Allie just ahead, not budging from her spot on the shoulder, the truck headed straight for her. "Allie!" I screamed. There were only a few feet to spare. She whipped her handlebars to the right, but her wheel slid in an arc into the ditch. Her tire couldn't get enough traction to stick and she slid sideways, down into the ditch—on her leg, foot clipped into the pedal, through the gravelly cinders and weeds. Her helmet hit dirt.

The truck drove right through the spot where Allie had been, the front wheel eight inches from her head. One wheel slipped off the shoulder, losing traction. For a horrifying moment I thought the truck might tip over on Allie, but it dug its tires in and spun out, gouging into the soft earth, spraying us both with gravel, cinders, and dirt.

The passenger stuck his head out of the window and yelled, "Get off the road! You'll get yours now, you little—" But I couldn't hear the rest. A beer bottle sailed out like an exclamation point.

Allie ducked and the bottle glanced off her helmet, hit her shoulder, and splattered her jersey with urine-colored liquid.

"Assholes!" she screamed.

The truck revved, and loud ugly laughs rolled over us. It spun off, sending another spray of gravel from the shoulder over Allie. Gravel bounced off her helmet and her sunglasses, and one rock hit her in the cheek.

"You ASSES!" she screamed. The truck roared away over the hill, and swerved as if it didn't anticipate the sharp turn on the crest of the hill. Tires squealed on the corner, but there was no crash. They'd made it around the bend upright.

"You ASSHOLES!" Allie screamed once more. She lifted her hand to her cheek and her fingers came back bloody.

"Are you okay?" I jumped over to her, grabbed her chin so I could look at her wound.

She jerked her face away from my fingers. "Fine. Let's go. It's gonna be frickin' dark."

❌❌

It was pretty dark by the time we pulled up to Scout's Last Chance. Allie practically had steam blowing out her ears. The first thing I noticed was Thomas's truck parked out front. Minus the cannon trailer. We hadn't seen him since the uncles got out of jail.

"Look!" Allie pointed to the blue, flag-flying pickup, parked two trucks down from Thomas's.

"Your uncle here?" she asked.

"Probably. He always is since he got out of the slammer."

"We're goin' in," she said.

She parked her bike against the wall of the bar and grill and marched up to the front door without even greeting Peapod. I quick parked my bike and followed. She yanked the wooden door open so hard it bounced off the outside wall.

Allie stood framed in the doorway, in her silver helmet, bug-like cycling glasses, and earrings, all her facial rings hanging out, with her fluorescent green jersey, black shorts, and lean tan legs so curved and muscled they could make most men swoon on the spot, with blood trickling down her cheek and her skinned leg. "Where *are* they, Scout?"

"Who?" Scout moved from behind the counter toward her. Thomas whirled around on his bar stool to face us.

Allie stepped inside and I followed. She whipped off her helmet and glasses and tossed them onto a pool table. She shook her white hair, ran one hand through it so it stood up, and scanned the room for the two rednecks. It was impossible to miss Allie's entrance, but the two guys were sitting in a booth on the far wall, so they didn't see who she was right away.

Allie spied them just as they realized who she was. One of them had the gall to lift a beer bottle in salute toward us. Allie said nothing. She snaked out her arm, snatched the cue ball off the pool table, and threw it so fast and hard I didn't realize what had happened until there was a crash across the room dwarfed only by my memory of the cannon explosion.

"How's that, you assholes?" she yelled, and charged them.

The white ball had lodged in the wood paneling inches in front of the pickup driver's nose. It had hit the bill of his black Schlitz cap, knocked it off, and gone right into the wall and stayed.

"Ohmygosh," I heard myself say.

Scout moved so fast two tables turned over. Ketchup bottles and napkin holders clanged to the floor and bounced. "Whoa, little lady." Scout stepped in front of her and caught her by the shoulder. "Whoa."

"Lady?" She shook him off.

He caught both shoulders and held on. "You just put a hole in my wall."

"And they tried to kill us!"

Scout looked from Allie to me.

Allie struggled in Scout's grip. "They drove off the road to try to hit us! We both hit the ditch or they'd have killed us."

"What the hell? Watch it!" The driver, now hatless, his collar-length hair matted from his cap, tried not to look shaken. He took a swig of his beer. "Bikes. Shouldn't be on the damn road at all." He was skinny except for a beer belly. Allie had lots more muscle than he did. "Road's for goddam *cars and trucks.*"

Allie pointed. "And *he* hit me with a beer bottle!"

"I wasn't tryin' to hit you," the other guy said to Allie. He wore his hair in a long greasy ponytail under a Vikings cap. His pointy face, without much chin, reminded me of a reptile. "You just got in the way of my bottle." Both men erupted in laughter, and clinked their bottles together in a drunken toast.

Scout looked over Allie's shoulder at me, standing limp by the door. He saw grass stains and sweaty dirt, but no blood. "Sadie? You okay?"

I nodded.

Scout turned to face the two and drew himself to full height, still holding Allie's arm. Thomas appeared behind Scout.

"Them bikes," the ponytail reptile guy said, "they were hoggin' the road and they wouldn't move over."

"That's a bunch of crap! We have a legal right to be on the road!" Allie yelled. "And we were way over on the shoulder, and they left a big tire track *off the road* where they *tried* to hit me."

Behind Scout, Thomas folded his arms over his ample stomach. I could see him flexing so his football-sized biceps stood out against the sides of his chest.

Scout moved toward the two men, who leaned away from him in the booth. "You two," Scout said. "You're outta here. NOW. You ever set foot in here again, you're dead meat."

"What about our food? We didn't even get our burgers. And we're not done with our beer. Besides, that little bitch almost hit me with a fuckin' pool ball."

"You weren't listening, were you?" I'd never heard Scout sound so patient. Or so deadly. Like a rattlesnake ready to strike. "I said you'd be dead meat, and I meant dead. If I called the cops right now, they'd slap a $200 fine on you for littering. Just for starters. But cops don't like coming to LeHillier, so I'd rather just kill you. Understand? So get out."

He flipped his head in Allie's direction. "She'll eat your burger for you. I don't want your stinkin' money for the beer. Now get out. And if you try anything, you hurt my niece, your ass *will* be dead. Did I say *dead* again? I meant dead. And I have just the fillet knife to do it."

They didn't budge, but they were frowning, and now they looked scared.

"Come on," the hatless, watery-blue-eyed driver said, getting up. "I think he means it."

"You're a tiny bit smarter than I thought," Scout said. He finally let go of Allie, grabbed the reptile ponytail guy by the front of his shirt and lifted him out of the booth. The guy's Vikings hat slid sideways. "Don't come back," Scout said.

The hatless driver lunged at Scout, ready to punch. Still holding the reptilian guy, Scout moved one foot so quickly, I only saw a blur. He tripped the hatless guy, who was so drunk he landed on the floor next to Thomas's feet. "You forgot your hat," Scout said. "Get it while you're down there. Don't leave it on my floor. I run a clean establishment."

The guy looked up at both huge men. His eyes narrowed, like he'd spit at them if he had the nerve.

"Get under there, you wimp," Thomas said, taking a step toward him. "Get your hat."

The hatless driver reached around the bench seat for his Schlitz cap, smashed it onto his head, and stood up.

"Now, get out. Don't *ever*, don't *ever* come back." Scout pointed to the door.

And they went.

Peapod, sprawled at his post outside the door, rose to his feet and growled so loudly the sound rumbled around the bar. The rest of the customers around the bar clapped.

We stood there, limp. Thomas wiped his face with his hanky. We could hear gravel spraying the side of the building as the truck took off.

Scout shook his head and pulled out a cigar.

Only then did I notice the kid sitting at the bar with a black shock of hair hanging over one eye. Now his mouth was hanging open. The kid from the gas pumps at the Blue Ox this morning.

"Oh, I almost forgot," Uncle Scout said. "Meet Joe."

"Joe?" I swallowed hard.

In my filthy, grassy spandex, with my stinky, mucky, sweat-covered body, my bike helmet and filthy face, I stuck out my hand. "Hi. I'm Sadie."

TWELVE

Joe

"Hi," Joe said back to me, shaking my hand. My hand was covered in a thin film of dirt. He looked me up and down and grinned. "Sadie. Aunt Susan told me about you. But nothing this interesting."

"Oh, great." I said, feeling bright red under all the dirt. "This is Allie."

"I figured," he said, and shook her hand, too.

"Come over and look at this." Thomas interrupted us from the rednecks' vacated booth. "Holy smoke, girl, you have some arm."

We all moved across the room to examine the ball lodged in the paneling. I was all too aware of Joe moving across the room right beside me.

"Holy crap," Joe said.

Thomas reached out to touch Allie's biceps in admiration.

She jerked her arm away, a reflex at his touch.

He dropped his hand. "Sorry."

She shrugged. "Sorry about the wall, Scout. Want me to pay for it?"

Scout shook his head. "Are you kidding? I'm gonna leave it there. Forever. Now wash up and we'll feed you."

In the restroom, Allie and I scrubbed our faces, hands, and arms. She wiped down her skinned leg, then examined her cheek in the mirror. "Not too bad."

"Want me to go find you a band-aid?"

"Naw." She shook her head. "Battle scars are cool." She grinned at me.

We slid onto bar stools, and my heart skittered when Joe moved his root beer over so he could take the bar stool next to mine.

Scout brought us the burgers, and a mountain of fries. I hadn't enjoyed red meat much since I'd started working at the Blue Ox, but I was starving and this tasted like heaven. Allie chowed through hers, too.

Scout kept all of our mugs full of root beer. I was so hungry, I wasn't even self-conscious eating in front of Joe.

Finally Joe broke the silence. "Sadie, I'd swear I've seen you before."

I swallowed so much burger and bun, I coughed. Finally I choked out, "Yeah. At the Blue Ox."

"Huh?"

"The truck stop. Where you got gas this morning."

"Oh…" He nodded, remembering. "That's it. You were at the cash register."

I nodded, still coughing and trying to swallow properly.

"You okay?" He grinned and patted me on the back. His touch was like electricity, and I felt my face go beet red.

"You brought a mountain bike." I said. "You ride a lot?"

"Yeah," he said. "And I hate redneck drivers, too. I'd rather be on trails where there aren't cars. I couldn't handle being a roadie. If somebody did that to me"—he nodded at us—"I'd want to kill 'em."

"I do want to," Allie said. "Didn't you notice?" She popped three ketchup-soaked French fries into her mouth.

"I thought it looked like you wanted to miss, with that dead-eye aim," Joe said.

"I *wanted* to kill 'em. I *tried* to knock his hat off," she said with her mouth full of fries. "You race?"

"Yeah, a little," Joe said. "Sport class."

"There're races here," Allie said. "Great big local race on the Fourth of July. And there's a NORBA race later in July. And a bunch in the Twin Cities."

"NORBA? What's that?" I asked.

"The National Off-Road Biking Association," Joe answered.

"Fourth of July race is at Mount Kato—outside of Mankato, not too far from here," Allie said. She looked at me. "Sadie's doin' it. Her first race ever."

"That's what *you* say," I said. "I haven't paid my entry fee or anything yet."

"You're doin' it. You'll be fine." Allie leaned toward me and whispered, "Ridin' through the chicken. Remember?"

I wondered how well Joe could ride, since he smoked and all. Instead of arguing more with Allie, I asked him, "What's the ladder for? In your trunk."

"I paint ... houses, porches, rooms ... anything. It's been my summer job since last year, so I brought my stuff. Thought I'd get some work that way. Gotta make some money this summer."

"Where are you from?" Allie asked.

"Phoenix."

"Great mountain biking in Phoenix," Allie said. "So why are you *here*?"

The fries sort of stuck in my throat.

Joe traced the sweat outline of his root-beer mug on the counter, slowly, around and around with an index finger. Any trace of what I thought was a swagger at the Blue Ox had wilted.

When the quiet got uncomfortable, Scout cleared his throat and said, "He just—"

Joe interrupted. "It's okay, Scout. My parents wanted me to get away. In February my twin brother died. I don't know if my parents wanted to get rid of me for the summer so I wouldn't keep reminding them of him, or if they wanted me to go away and stop thinking about it. But—whatever—they sent me here. I agreed only if they'd let me drive up alone and bring my bike and my painting stuff."

"Sorry," Allie said. "What happened … I mean, to your brother?"

Now I wished I'd pumped Mom for more information. Aunt Susan had said it was a "horrible accident." I imagined a flaming car and a kid trapped inside, a car smashed by a semi-truck. A kid on a bike smashed by a swerving pickup. Horrible accidents. A stray cannonball that blew up a parked motorcycle didn't seem so bad.

"Hiking accident," Joe said.

That didn't explain much, but his answer closed the subject. I couldn't quite imagine a horrible accident hiking. A bad fall? Cougar attack?

We chewed, swallowed. The place stayed quiet. I tried to study Joe's face without looking directly at him. He'd seemed so cool and mature or something at the Blue Ox. Now I wondered if some of what I saw was just sadness.

"So," Thomas said, forcing brightness into his voice. "On the Fourth of July, Scout and I will be doing a Civil War re-enactment in the parade, and we'll shoot a Civil War Cannon during Rockin' in the Quarry." *Effective diversion*, I thought, and it was working. "You kids will have to come watch after your race."

"They're gonna let you shoot your cannon again?" I asked.

"The cannon, my dear," Thomas said with a grand sweep of his hand, "has been relegated to ornamental uses, like parades and reenactments. I swore to Janie on the Bible. And to my lawyer, too. Only official capacities."

Scout winked at me. "We might think of all sorts of official capacities."

I couldn't keep from laughing, then. "What's Rockin' in the Quarry?"

"The Mankato Symphony puts on a concert in a huge limestone quarry. They play the *1812 Overture* and we fire the cannon at the appropriate time in the music."

"Oh, great," I said. "What can you blow up in there?"

Both big boys chuckled, shook their heads. Scout said, "That's the point of having it in the quarry. Nothing. Besides, we shoot oatmeal cannonballs."

"By the way," I said, "speaking of that, why did Janie let you out of the house? I figured she hadn't let you out of her sight since you got out of jail."

Thomas grinned out of one side of his mouth and wiped his face with his hanky. "She's gone. At her mom's, overnight with the kids. Plus"—here he held up his mug—"only root beer to drink." I knew Scout hadn't touched a drop of alcohol all summer, either.

"What's this about?" Joe asked. He winked at me. I could barely tear my eyes away from his face.

We told Joe the story of Memorial Day.

He laughed. "Holy crap. That's not quite the way my mom heard it from Aunt Susan."

"Be careful bringing it up around Aunt Susan," I said. "It's a very sore subject."

Joe gave me a lopsided grin. "I s'pose. I think I won't even mention it."

"Good man." Scout stood up. "Well, you kids should probably skedaddle. I have to coddle my other customers. This is a bar, after all. Miss Strong-Arm Allie, if you ever need refuge from another redneck storm, consider yourself welcome here. I'd be honored if you'd count me as your friend."

Allie shook Uncle Scout's and Uncle Thomas's hands.

THIRTEEN

Joe and Allie

June 15

Joe got a job painting with a group of teachers who always paint in the summer. Uncle Scout hooked him up, his first morning in LeHillier. So Joe worked from seven a.m. until four every day. He was sleeping in Scout's study, near the gun cabinet and in the midst of heavy cigar scent. The study was less private, but had more atmosphere than my sewing closet. The only time I saw him much was at dinner.

✖✖

When I told Barb at the Blue Ox about Joe, she said, "You be careful with him, Sadie Lester. I still say there's something dark inside that boy."

I smiled. "Guess I'll find out."

I grabbed six coffee cups, a pot of coffee, my pad and pen, and put on a smile and went to work.

June 18

At dinner a few nights later, Joe asked me, "Ride today? How long? Where'd you go?" After I answered, he was quiet except when somebody asked him a question. I wanted to just hang out with him, but I didn't know how to ask. He disappeared after the meal to go have a smoke, and I don't know where he went after that.

The next night, I asked him, "You want Allie and me to ride at four thirty so you can go with us?"

"Would you?"

"Can't get ahold of Allie now, but tomorrow, I'll ask her about the next day."

So Allie and I waited to ride until four thirty in the afternoon so Joe could go with us. Allie still wouldn't tell me where she lived or give me a phone number. I stopped asking.

Joe wasn't a bad rider. He got winded quickly, which wasn't surprising, I guess, considering how much he smoked. The weirdest thing about him was that he froze at the top of tricky descents before he could force himself to let go of the brakes and *go*. It was almost a freaky fear. Otherwise, he was a decent bike handler.

June 23

The third time Joe rode with us, his cell phone rang. He slowed down, fished it out of his jersey pocket, and answered it.

Allie charged ahead, not waiting for him. I followed her. When he finally hung up and caught back up almost a mile later, she said, "You don't bring a goddam cell phone when you ride mountain bike. If you can't go without civilization, stay home."

"Sorry," Joe said. "Holy crap, I didn't think it would be such a big deal. It's for emergencies."

"Bullshit," she said. "Why'd you answer it then?"

After a three-and-a-half hour ride, including Embolism Hill where Joe fell way behind Allie and me, we pulled into SuperAmerica in Mankato and bought giant cherry slushies. We leaned our bikes against the building and sat on the curb, dusty, grimy, sweaty, and thirsty, sucking down the sweet ice.

"Cell phone's bad enough," Allie said, digging for cherry syrup at the bottom of her tall paper cup, "but how come you smoke?"

"It relaxes me. And pretty much everybody in my school smokes." Joe took a big gulp of icy juice. "And I like it. How come you don't?"

"So I can ride fast, you moron. And so I don't screw up the air for everybody else. And it costs a fortune, too."

"At my school, the only guys who don't smoke are endurance athletes, like distance runners or swimmers."

"You're a mountain biker. Doesn't that mean anything to you?"

Joe shrugged. "All the artsy kids, musicians, theater geeks, everybody smokes."

"So are you artsy? What else do you do?"

"Oh, I play bari-sax. I like Jazz band best. I like jazz. I'm not too bad at it, but I'd like to be really good. And I jump in track—long jump, high jump. I'm not any good, but I like going out for it. Smoking doesn't matter if you jump."

"It matters on your bike," Allie said.

"I haven't heard you play your sax," I said, hoping to change the subject and save Joe.

"It's in Scout's study." He looked at me, and my heart sort of twitched. "There's not exactly air space in that house to make music. You like jazz?"

"Yeah, I do, actually. I love blues. If you played, I'd listen. You could probably play in my sewing closet. There's so much fabric in there, it'd muffle the sound."

I could practically feel Allie rolling her eyes.

"Hmm," said Joe. "Maybe."

We were quiet.

"We don't smoke," Allie said. I looked at her, wondered why she brought it up again, and for a second I almost hated her for badgering Joe so much.

"I noticed," Joe said, staring at the pavement.

"It affects your riding. Have you noticed that?"

"As a matter of fact, yeah. I notice when I ride with you two. Never noticed before. Not with anybody I ride with."

"You'll notice when you race. Around here, you won't have a chance with shitty lungs."

"I was afraid of that."

"So quit."

"Riding?"

"Smoking, idiot."

"Can't stop just *like that*. And … I like it. It tastes good. And it relaxes me, like I said."

Allie jumped to her feet. "That's such bullshit. Bullshit. You know how many times I hear that excuse? *'Oh, sorry, can't stop. Just can't help myself. You don't know what it's like to be addicted …'* To cigarettes, to pot, to sex, to booze, to soap operas, to the frickin' Internet, to gambling. To crack, to meth … It's all the same excuse. It's *bullshit*. You decide how you want to live and you *do* it. You wanna smoke, be a smoker. But frickin' *stop* if you want to keep riding with us. I won't wait for you on the hills anymore if you're still smoking." She jumped up, threw the rest of her slushie in the trash, and grabbed her bike. "If you quit, I'll wait for you any day, anywhere, and I'll bust my ass to help you get faster, but I'm not sitting waiting for somebody to catch up who can't keep up 'cause he's ruining his own lungs!" She threw her leg over her bike. "Or 'cause he's on the goddam cell phone!"

"Allie!" I said. "Chill out. What's with you? Let him be!"

"It's okay," Joe said. "I just think she doesn't want me riding with you."

"No, you moron. You smoke-sucking idiot," Allie said. "I like you, don't you get it? If I didn't like you, I wouldn't give a rat's ass. But I do, so I don't want to see you die of lung cancer or blow your chances at being really *good* on the bike. You are—you could be. But that extra lung power for the big climbs? You'll never have it. You won't have anything. Except maybe an early coffin or a hind-end view of the guys ahead of you, who dropped you 'cause they *don't* smoke. So decide."

"Holy crap, calm down," Joe said. "Sorry."

"Sorry? *Sorry?*" Allie glared at him. "Don't be sorry to me. They're your lungs. And, while I'm at it, what's with this *holy crap* bullshit? Why don't you swear and get it over with? Too holy or something to swear, but not too holy to wreck your own body?" And she was on her bike and starting to pedal.

"How do you really feel?" Joe said to her disappearing backside. She flipped up her middle finger behind her back and accelerated away.

"Holy crap," Joe said. He looked so deflated, I felt my own heart sinking a little. He sure wasn't the Hollywood-cool tough guy he'd appeared to be at the Blue Ox. He was just a guy. Still sexy as all get-out, but just an ordinary guy. I ached for him. And for some crazy reason, the more I got to know him, the more I wanted to kiss those lips. But now I couldn't stop thinking about what Allie had said, and it made me sad and mad.

"I think she likes you," I said.

"I don't think so," Joe said. "I think she likes *you*. Maybe that means she hates me a little bit 'cause she's jealous. And she sort of hates the world and is taking it out on me. And smoking is just her excuse."

"Hates the world? Jealous? She said she likes you. My impression is," I said, "that Allie says exactly what she means. She thinks you can be good. If she says she likes you, she does. I don't think she bullshits anybody. She doesn't want you to screw up your chances on the bike. Or maybe screw up your life."

Joe just looked at me.

"Wait." I chewed my lip. "What did you mean? When you said maybe she's jealous? *Jealous?*"

"Maybe she likes *you* and she's jealous of me, doesn't want to share you with me."

"Share me?" I stared at him and my heart thumped. "What are you talkin' about?"

"She had you all to herself before I showed up."

"So?" My heart hammered with a little bit of hope that Joe might be feeling what I was feeling. That maybe he meant Allie was jealous that Joe liked me.

"Don't you think she's a dyke?" he asked. "I think she *likes* you. Didn't you see how she jerked away that day at the Last Chance when Thomas just *touched* her?"

"Well, we'd just gotten creeped out. That was really scary. I was jumpy, too."

Joe shrugged. "Not like that. She doesn't like to be touched, at least by a guy, that's for sure."

"We were both freaked out. That doesn't mean she's a—shouldn't you say '*lesbian*'?"

"Maybe not," Joe said. "But I still say she *likes* you. And she doesn't want to share you with me."

I jumped to my feet. "I can't believe you said that."

"Don't get all defensive. What? Are you sayin' that you like her that way, too? And I walked into the middle of it? Sorry."

"Joe, I *like* her a lot, too, but it doesn't mean I *want* her. Or that she *wants* me." I grabbed my bike. "I really don't believe you said that. What makes you think—?" I stared at him, wondering if I'd misinterpreted every little sign that maybe he liked me. "I thought you were a decent guy. That's sort of twisted. We're just friends."

Before he got up from the curb, I was riding away, leaving him sitting with his stupid slushie.

❉❉

That night at supper, I didn't talk to Joe. I caught him looking at me a couple times, but after we ate, he took his saxophone out to the edge of the woods and played for the first time. He was good. Really good. The notes were sweet and lingered on the evening air. The music was sad, like the sadness I saw behind his eyes sometimes. It made me want to cry. For him, for me, for Allie. I also didn't see him go out for his last cigarette before bed.

I went into my CCC closet and found the blues on my iPod that I downloaded at Dad's last Christmas.

What the heck. Why did this have to be complicated? Allie a lesbian? It hadn't crossed my mind. I just liked her.

She was the most interesting friend I'd ever had. When we rode, I wanted to *be* her.

If she was lesbian, so what? And Allie jealous? That was the stupidest thing I'd ever heard. But why would Joe even think about that? Did it mean maybe he liked me? Could it? That he thought Allie was jealous of him and me? Impossible. He was...sexy, in spite of not being the tough guy I thought he was. He was...beautiful. I was plain ol' me with a stupid brown ponytail. A chicken. Who couldn't ever think of the right thing to say. Who sat by listening while they fought. And now I'd blown up at him, too, and probably ruined my chances forever. Stupid, stupid, stupid me.

I fell asleep to sad muted trumpet on my iPod.

FOURTEEN
Fear Factor

June 29

After Joe moved in, there were simply too many people in too small a space. The tension in the house grew, then settled like dust. Too many of us moving all at once stirred it up, but most of the time we could ignore it. I chose to stay outside—on my bike, walking Peapod—or in my CCC closet whenever I didn't have to work, either at the Blue Ox or for Aunt Susan. Joe smoked outside, and went who knows where. He had a car, after all. After Allie blew up at him, he played his sax sometimes and avoided me. He didn't ride with us anymore and quit talking to me at all. He seemed exempt from all the household tasks Aunt Susan gave me. I didn't know if she let him off easy because he was a boy, or her own nephew, or in mourning for his brother, or working full-time. No matter what her reason was, it pissed me off. But of course I couldn't complain about it.

Timmy was oblivious. The highlight of his life was living with his cousin Stevie for the summer. Allie was the only one I could talk to, and somehow it seemed wrong to complain to her about Joe and make that whole scene any worse. So I said nothing.

I felt like Cedar Claustrophobia Central was the perfect name for my summer, except for riding with Allie.

⁌ ⁌

When I got home from work one day, I stopped in the Last Chance before going to the house. Peapod was all wags and giant happy tongue to greet me. He weighed over a hundred pounds, which was huge even for a lab mix, so a hundred pounds of wag could be lethal. He flopped back on the cement when I ducked into the bar.

"Hi, Scout."

"Sadie. What's up?"

"What happened to Joe's brother hiking? How did he die?"

Scout chewed his unlit cigar. He handed me a root beer. Root beer was his ambrosia, the healing potion for all ills. "I think Joe should be the one to tell you that. It's his story, not mine."

"If I'd been paying attention when I heard that you and Aunt Susan went to a funeral in Arizona, I'd have found out then. But I wasn't paying attention."

"I'm not gonna tell you because I think Joe might need to do that, even if he hasn't yet. You'll pay attention now, I bet. When he's ready to talk."

I drained my mug. "Thanks for the root beer, Scout," I said, heading for the door. "Peapod, want to go for a walk?"

Peapod leaped to his feet with full-body wags.

Megan was watching *Beauty and the Beast* for the millionth time, so I snuck past her. Peapod waited for me in the kitchen while I changed into shorts and then bounded ahead of me down the trail toward the river, looking more like a sleek lion than a peapod, only slowing to jump higher than the grass to see me, to make sure I was following him.

Near the bottom, where the trail fanned out into clay and sand, he stopped, mid-stride, skidding, and the fur on his scruff bristled. He froze in a point position.

"What is it, Peapod?" I said, barely louder than a whisper. I could hear the approaching hum of four-wheeler ATVs on the path. Peapod bolted back to me and leaned against me, growling toward the motor. I grabbed his collar and pulled him off the path, into the woods about ten feet.

Three four-wheelers, the recreational vehicle of choice in this neck of the woods, came barreling closer, going way too fast, spraying dirt, and Peapod kept growling. The dirt came raining down on us, even from ten feet away.

I couldn't figure out the growling, since Peapod always hung out on the front sidewalk of Scout's Last Chance, greeting customers. Too lazy to get up most of the time, he'd just lie there on his side and wag, even when the local riffraff came and went. The only time I'd ever heard him growl was at the two rednecks from the blue pickup.

I hung onto Peapod and watched. The four-wheelers came zipping past, and I felt my breath suck in like a punch. The guy in front was wearing a helmet, but a familiar long greasy ponytail flopped out behind. The reptile guy. I was surprised the ponytail didn't leave a grease streak down his back. The second guy, without a helmet, was the driver of the pickup, wearing his black Schlitz cap backwards.

Peapod had been running a low-grade growl, but when the third four-wheeler zipped even with us, he let out a full-fledged snarl and almost yanked his collar out of my hand.

The snarl was so loud, the driver guy and the third guy heard it over the roar of their motors. The Schlitz-cap guy slowed way down and leered a half-grin at me. Recognition spread over his skinny, bristly face, and then the grin slid off his face and his eyes narrowed.

I'd never seen the third guy before. He wore pale green sunglasses and a short haircut under a Polaris Snowmobile cap. His face was handsome in a worn sort of way, full of chiseled lines, like wrinkled leather. His body looked hard and his arms were tight as thick rope.

Peapod lunged right at him and almost ripped my arm out of its socket. He jerked me forward and went crazy, snarling and snapping. Way worse than he'd growled at the two rednecks from the pickup.

The man looked unperturbed. He saw us, all right. He barely turned his head as he slowed down to stare at us. Even through his sunglasses, his gaze was hard as cold steel, boring holes into me. He looked as if he'd as soon squash Peapod as veer from his course. A steel, leather, and ice man. He gave me the chills. And Peapod hated him.

The driver guy, putting along really slow now, looked over his shoulder at the Polaris guy and indicated me with a tilt of his head. Then he gunned his motor, and took off after the reptile guy in a dirt-flinging wheelie.

❌❌

After the noise died away in the woods, Peapod calmed down and I let him go. He trotted in the direction where the four-wheelers had disappeared, sniffed their tracks, and rumbled one more low growl. Then he charged down the rest of the hill and jumped in the river, but he only splashed around for about a minute before bounding out again to check on me.

Motors approached again, and Peapod had heard them before I did. No growl this time, but Peapod stepped between me and the trail. I hung onto his collar and watched. Two boys, maybe twelve years old, maybe four-teen, roared toward us and slowed when they saw us. They both nodded at me, and each one stood his machine on two wheels to spin out, accelerating a wheelie away from me.

I couldn't help laughing. "Oh yeah," I said aloud to their disappearing backs, "I'm really impressed." I rubbed Peapod's head and he jumped back into the river.

"Wanna go home?" I asked when I had walked far enough along the river to see the chain-saw sign hanging on its tree, starting to sag. Peapod wagged and started up the path. Sometimes I had to coax him out of the water, but today he didn't need coaxing.

Sure enough, we were almost at the top of the hill, when I could hear ATVs coming back toward us. "Peapod," I said, "come here." He came, and we hightailed it deeper into the woods. For once, the junk was a good thing. I squatted down behind an old refrigerator lying on its side and pulled Peapod after me. I made him sit so his tail wouldn't give us away. The noise came kiting down the hill. I was sure it was the same rednecks and their buddy, and that they would be watching for me. I ducked low.

Peapod's growl turned to a snarl before the motors even got close, so I pulled him closer and put my hands around his nose to shush him. I leaned out to look.

Sure enough, they were motoring back the way they'd come, and they were scouring the woods for the sight of me. My heart was hammering and Peapod strained against my hands, growling, but he let me hold him. Finally they gave up, revved their engines, and took off, bouncing away down the hill.

When they were out of sight, Peapod's hackles were still standing up more than I'd ever seen them. We ran as fast as we could back to the house. I hosed Peapod down to get the river water out of his coat. "Good boy," I said, rubbing his wet head. "Good boy." I couldn't imagine how creepy the third guy must be if he got such a rise out of Peapod. I took off my shoes and rinsed off my legs, too, using Scout's shop soap, in case there was poison ivy where we'd hidden.

Aunt Susan saw us from the garden where she had Josie "helping" her weed between tomato plants. Stevie and Timmy were picking peas. "Sadie! Will you go check on Stacie? She's sleeping in her crib. Then would you get Megan and both come help us pick peas?"

"Okay," I said. My heart still hadn't calmed down to normal speed, but I was hoping she didn't notice.

"Please," Aunt Susan added to my back, as if she'd just remembered. Of course she wouldn't notice. She could barely keep her nose above water.

Stacie was still sound asleep, and Megan, in the middle of *Beauty and the Beast* for the ten-thousandth time, complained about leaving Belle still in the grips of the Beast who hadn't turned nice yet, but she and I went out and helped with the pea-picking. I looked at Aunt Susan's tired face, and I knew I would never say anything to her about the guys in the woods.

We six pea-pickers ate about as many raw peas as we put in the bowl, and then I helped Susan weed carrots. My heart rate seemed back to normal now, but I couldn't get rid of the creeps.

Josie, who was playing in the grass beside the garden, started to whine. "Mommy, I want juice."

Susan let out a big sigh.

"Go ahead," I said. "I can finish these."

"Thanks." It was the first time I'd seen gratitude on her face, instead of frustration, all summer. She picked up Josie in one arm and the bowl of peas in the other. The boys took off for the fort they were building behind Scout's shop. Peapod lay down near the tomatoes and kept an eye on me while I finished.

We heard another ATV motor on the trail in the woods. Peapod looked at me and I looked at him. But he lay there, calmly, and I kept pulling weeds.

When I was done, I went to find Scout again. I let Peapod, who was almost dry now, in the back door of the Last Chance with me. "Scout?" I called. "Uncle Scout?" No answer. Peapod's claws clicked and my flip-flops padded over the tile floor. When we went into the bar itself, Peapod lay down in the doorway. The only light in the dark room was the glowing end of Scout's huge cigar. He was at a booth, sitting alone, staring out the tinted window.

"Scout?"

He jumped, so the ash fell off his cigar onto the table. He chomped down, brushed the ashes from the table into one palm, and grinned at me around the cigar.

"Caught me thinkin'," he said. "And smokin' in a public establishment."

"What are you thinking about?" I slid into the booth across from him.

He held his cigar with two fingers of the hand that wasn't holding the ashes. "Those two scumbags who chased you on your bikes. They rode by here today on ATVs. With some other scumbag. I'm not likin' that. They made a big circle around the whole place. I went out to tell 'em to get lost before I called the cops, but they took off like bats out of hell as soon as I opened the door."

"I saw them. Peapod and I were in the woods. Peapod growled like crazy. But the third guy? The one with them? I've never heard Peapod growl like that. And snarl. And snap. He would have ripped that guy's legs off if I'd let him go. Almost jerked my arm off."

Peapod, hearing his name, whined from the door.

"Come here, you big oaf," Scout said. Peapod wagged into the bar and Scout rubbed his ears.

"Then some kids went by, and Peapod didn't even care."

Uncle Scout studied my face while he rubbed the big golden head beside him. "Old gentle, ever-loving Peapod, you got more sense than I give you credit for."

"They heard Peapod, and they saw me. That last guy—it felt like he looked right through me. Scared the crap out of me. Peapod really hated him."

Scout pulled the cigar from his mouth and studied it. "No idea who that one was?"

I shook my head. "I was hoping you knew. Since Peapod hates him so much."

"No idea," Scout said, slowly turning his root beer mug in its sweat ring on the table. "Sure you've never seen him?"

I shook my head again. "Did you call the cops?"

"Yup, I did. I was hoping they'd mind their own business so we wouldn't have to. But I guess they aren't smart enough for that."

He paused.

"Sadie." Scout pointed the two fingers holding the cigar at me. "For now, don't go in the woods alone. Not even with Peapod, okay?"

I nodded.

✖✖

The policeman—a detective—showed up fifteen minutes later. Scout had given him instructions to pull up to the front of the bar and grill *without* lights or siren. He wanted to prevent Susan from seeing the cop car if possible.

The officer's name was Rankin. Scout asked him if that made him a rankin' officer. Rankin didn't crack a smile, just shook his head and started asking questions. No nonsense. I had to tell Officer Rankin the story about getting chased, and describe where it happened, including hitting the ditch, the pickup half off the road trying to hit us, the beer bottle hitting Allie, and seeing the guys today.

"You say you don't know the guys?" he asked.

We both shook our heads.

"The girl with you know them? And what's her name again?"

I shook my head again. "I don't think so. She would have said...Allie—Allison Baker."

He made a couple notes in his notebook. "Let's go look at the road."

Uncle Scout nodded. "Come on. Sadie knows the spot."

He locked up Scout's Last Chance, stuck a *Back at 3:30* note on the door, and he and Peapod and I piled into his red and white pickup. We led the cop out to the hill where the jerks had run us into the ditch. The tire track was still there, deep and thick, hardened in the clay and dirt, and the marks farther up, at the curve in the road, were still visible, too.

The cop looked around carefully and wrote in his notebook. Then he pointed out a place where a mountain bike tire track was visible, intersecting the line of the pickup tread track, which blotted it out.

"Wow," I said. "That's Allie's track."

He looked around a little more, and then closely examined Scout's truck and tires. We watched him.

"I believe you," he said. "Sorry, but I had to check your tread against these tracks. Just to make sure you didn't make the track. Procedure. Not a match." He made a few more notes. "We'll see what we can do." He shook our hands. "Thanks for the info, Scout, Sadie."

We watched him drive away. Scout put his hand on my shoulder.

✖✖

When we got back, I heard saxophone notes floating from the woods. Joe was home early. I followed the sound out behind the house, leaned against a tree, and listened. I wondered how he could do that—make the music so full of emotion. It almost made me cry. I must have moved or sniffed or something, because Joe whipped around, surprised.

"You're good. Really good."

"Aw … not really. But thanks."

I told him about the rednecks and the other freaky guy.

"That's messed up. I wonder what their deal is," he said, and we were quiet for a few minutes.

"Joe—" I said, "I'm sorry for Allie. For what she said."

"It's okay, Sadie. It's not your fault. I'm sorry for what I said, too. I didn't want to tick you off. I … " He scuffed a toe in the dead grass. "I haven't had a smoke since. I start to light up, and all I can see is your face when Allie was yellin' at me."

"*My* face? You mean *her* face?"

"No, your face. All horrified. I'm sorry you got stuck in the middle." He tossed the hair out of his eyes. "I felt worse for you than for me. You looked so sad. And so pretty."

I stared at him. "What—what did you say?"

"You heard me, didn't you?"

I nodded, but I couldn't say anything. He just looked at me and my heart hammered.

Finally, I stammered, "So...so, you want to ride with us? We're going tomorrow at four thirty."

He smiled, shrugged. "Not sure Allie wants me."

"I'll go first. Tell her you haven't smoked. I'll tell her I invited you. She's always on time, so come five minutes late. If we're still there, it's fine with her."

"Sadie?"

"Yeah?"

"Thanks."

FIFTEEN

Winds and Rain

June 30

At 4:25 on Saturday afternoon, I was sitting on the Last Chance front step, mountain bike leaning on the wall behind me, waiting for Allie and watching dark storm clouds gather, starting to boil on the western horizon.

"Hey." Allie skidded up to me in her usual fashion. Peapod wagged over to her and flopped back down.

"I invited Joe," I said.

She narrowed her eyes at me.

"He hasn't had a cigarette since you yelled at him."

"Serious?"

I nodded.

She shrugged. "Okay, I guess." She rubbed Peapod without looking at me until Joe pulled up on his bike.

"Hey," was all she said to him before she threw her leg over her bike and headed out.

Joe hesitated, one foot on the ground, one on his pedal, and looked at me. "You sure this is okay?"

"Absolutely." I grinned at him and nodded toward Allie's back. "Today, we won't let her drop us."

We rode west so we could keep an eye on the storm. It was rolling in fast, so we only rode out for forty-five minutes and turned around.

The rain clouds closed in. We rode three abreast on a deserted gravel road. Allie didn't say anything about smoking, but she teased Joe about the paint splatters on his neck and arms that he hadn't scrubbed off. She said he'd get a leopard-spot tan.

We laughed, and it felt good. Joe relaxed more and more the farther we rode. But then, it's hard to stay tensed up when you're riding for all you're worth.

I said, "I saw the guys from the blue pickup in the woods yesterday."

Allie's head jerked up. "No shit."

I told her the whole story, including the Polaris-cap guy and the detective, and Allie frowned.

"Peapod's no dummy," Joe said.

"What did the third guy look like?" Allie asked.

I'd started to describe him and his arms like rawhide when a few fat drops pelted our arms and helmets, hard as BBs. "Never mind!" Allie yelled over the wind. "Let's go!" And she down-shifted and took off. Joe and I followed.

By the time we reached LeHillier, the wind and the rain were pounding us.

"Wanna come in?" I yelled to Allie through the downpour, outside Scout's.

"No, thanks. This looks like it'll last awhile. I'm already drenched, so I better just go home."

"Sunday tomorrow. I don't have to work, do you?" I hollered.

"No," they both said.

"Let's ride at nine," Allie said. "Okay?"

"Sure. Want to give me your number where I can call you just in case?" My voice was getting drowned out in thunder.

She stopped, rain running off her helmet, making rivulets down her arms. "It's not worth it. Mom's *always* on the Internet. And we only have dial-up."

"We can ride over and pick you up. Just tell us where," Joe yelled. He was standing under the Last Chance entry, squeezing water out of his jersey.

"No!" she said. "I'll just be here at nine."

I shrugged. "Whatever. Okay, see you at nine. Be careful."

And she took off.

✖✖

Joe and I sprinted through the downpour to put our bikes in the garage. Once inside the house, we started stripping off whatever wet clothes we could spare while staying decent. "Holy crap, these are heavy," he said holding his shoes. Our soaked shoes and socks weighed about five pounds apiece.

Joe peeled off his jersey. His chest was cut, tan. He truly was beautiful, and completely unaware that I was staring at his body. "I'm sure glad I don't have to go out in the rain to get a smoke, tonight."

When he looked up, I tried to act like I wasn't staring.

"Nobody ever quite put it like Allie did," he continued. "I just figured I'd quit sometime when I needed to. I don't want to smoke for the rest of my life, but it's no big deal now, ya know? I was dyin' at work these last days, I wanted a cigarette so bad. I was praying to just get through the day." He grinned again. "I chewed three packs of gum and drank a whole case of Mountain Dew in two days." He laughed and rubbed his wet jersey on his cold, wet chest.

I tried to keep my eyes on his face while looking at his chest, but I wasn't doing a very good job of it.

"But," he went on, "I threw the cigs away that afternoon when I was so ticked off at Allie. I felt like *well, I'll show her.*"

"Good for you," I said.

"Oh, shut up." He gave my shoulder a gentle shove. "It's only been a few days. And it's only to prove to her that I can, 'cause she made me so mad." He smiled. I felt the nearness of his naked chest and I forgot about being cold and wet.

"I bet Allie did that on purpose. To make you so mad you'd quit," I said. "And your lungs probably don't care why you quit."

He leaned over and gently grabbed my ponytail and pulled my face close to his. "Thanks for asking me to ride again." My heart thundered, and there we stood, our faces an inch apart.

"Let's go shower," he whispered. "I'm freezing."

He let go of my hair, and I followed him into the kitchen. I tiptoed to the bathroom so I wouldn't leave big wet footprints. I threw Joe a bath towel and shut myself in to take a hot shower. Joe went to the basement bathroom.

I stood leaning on the shower wall, letting the water run over me, breasts, hips, legs, trying to calm my heart from thundering like the sky outside.

After we'd both showered, we met in the kitchen to find leftovers from dinner. Aunt Susan refused to wait dinner on us when we were out riding, so we lived on leftovers. We were starving, and wolfed down chicken and cold steamed asparagus.

"So what do you know about Allie?" Joe asked me, his mouth full of chicken thigh meat.

"That she can kick my butt any day of the week."

"Besides that. I mean, why won't she give you her phone number or anything?"

I shook my head. "She doesn't say much about herself." My heart thumped the same way it had when Joe'd said he thought Allie hadn't wanted to share me with him. I thought about Allie's dad in prison, but that seemed private, like something she'd trusted me with that I shouldn't tell anybody else. "Why?" I asked. "What do you want to know? You like her?"

"You mean, like, want her? Like a girlfriend? You nuts? She'd rip a guy's heart out and eat it for lunch. Besides..." He leaned across the table. "Who could see her with you around?"

"Me?"

"Sadie. You're...amazing."

I knew I was smiling. A warm glow spread all through my insides. It was the first time all summer I was thoroughly glad to be me, to live in my own skin.

"Don't get mad at me for saying this," Joe said. "Promise?"

"Can't promise until I know what you're going to say."

"Think she's a dyke? I mean, seriously?"

I jumped up. "Why do you keep bringing that up?" Just when I felt so happy. Tears stung my eyes. "What's the deal?"

"You said that you wouldn't get mad."

"I didn't promise anything." I grabbed the container of chicken and slammed it back into the refrigerator. "What difference does it make? Why should it make any difference at all if she is?"

"Holy crap, settle down. Why are you so pissed when I bring that up?"

I wanted to say, *you bring her up almost every time I feel like you like me; whenever you're close to me, you're obviously thinking about her*, but I just said, "'Cause she's my friend! And..."

"And what? And so what if she is? It's not a horrible thing to be a lesbian. I have friends at school who are dykes. I just wondered. And I didn't ask if you were a dyke. Just her."

"Shut up."

"Why? Has she made a pass at you?" he asked.

"No!" I stared at him, trying to figure out if he was serious. His eyes were twinkling, but I could see that he meant his question. "Honestly? It *never* occurred to me. And shouldn't you say 'lesbian'?"

Joe shrugged. "She's cool. I like her, too. Doesn't matter to me. And I say 'dyke' 'cause my friends at school call *themselves* dykes. Or 'queer.' They call themselves queer mostly."

Timmy and Stevie came running into the kitchen, flying balsa-wood planes. Stevie launched one and it bonked into Joe's shoulder. "Watch it," Joe said. He picked it up and handed it back. "Better take those to the family room. Or the garage. Not so much stuff to crash into."

"Oh, yeah, the garage!" Timmy yelled, and off they went.

My mind was spinning. The "out" lesbians in my high school were militant. Loud. Highly pierced, with buzzed heads, clunky boots...Allie sort of fit the stereotype, but it wasn't something that mattered. I just liked her, and didn't think about it. In fact, I admired her so much I wanted to *be* her. Maybe that was the part that bugged me. I wanted to *be* her. I couldn't make all these pieces connect.

Joe watched the rain out the kitchen window and said, "If this was Arizona, we'd be flash-flooded right down the river."

"Why does it matter to you?" I said again.

"Flash floods?"

"You dork. If Allie's a lesbian."

He shrugged. "Just want to know where I stand."

I squinted at him, trying to figure out what he meant. He smiled slowly at me. "Want to know my competition. 'Night, Sadie." He went into the study and shut the door.

I made myself a cup of mint tea and sat in the kitchen, listening to the thunder and watching the lightning for a long time. I really, really wished Erica or Sara were online to IM or at least email. But even with a slim chance that they were online, Scout's computer was in the office with Joe. Nobody to talk to about Joe.

I took my tea down to Cedar Claustrophobia Central and curled up on the fold-out with the latest issue of *Bicycling* magazine. At least Mom had forwarded my mail for the summer. Of course, I couldn't read or sleep. Even in this insulated cellar, I could hear the wind howling and feel Joe's hand on my ponytail.

SIXTEEN

Finding Father

July 1

I must have fallen asleep reading because my light was still on when Joe woke me at eight fifteen. When I opened my eyes, he was leaning over my fold-out bed. "Sadie! You better get up if we're meeting Allie at nine."

"It's morning? Oh, hi."

Joe reached out his hand as if he wanted to touch my hair, but then pulled it back. "Meet you upstairs."

We ate oatmeal and drank orange juice. I poured cereal for Josie and got Stacie set up with a pile of Cheerios on her highchair tray. Timmy, Stevie, and Megan were already eating in front of cartoons.

"Thanks," Aunt Susan said. She looked frazzled already. "You riding *now?*"

"Yeah," I said.

"We're meeting Allie," Joe said.

I felt as if I should ask if it was okay that we went, but I couldn't quite bring myself to give her the option of saying no. I hadn't asked for permission all summer, and if she said no now, I'd feel obligated to stay home and help her. Then what about Allie?

"As soon as we get back," I said, "I'll do whatever you need, okay? Make a list." I smiled, hoping I looked helpful.

On the way out the door, Joe poked me with his elbow and muttered, "Brown-noser."

I elbowed back.

Allie's bike was parked by the front door of the Last Chance. She was waiting for us inside, sitting on the floor and rubbing Peapod.

"Be careful," Scout said. "Have fun. Stick together, will ya?" He put an unlit cigar in his mouth and started sweeping the bar floor. "Those assholes make me more than a little nervous. And there are lots of trees down from the storm. So be careful."

Allie, Joe, and I took off into the woods, bouncing our way over downed tree limbs and leaves.

※※

That's the morning Joe slid on the slick leaves and catapulted into the ravine. That's when we found Father Malcolm, his body beaten to a barely breathing, bloody pulp in the woods.

※※

When Allie rode off to call 911, all Joe and I could do was wait, sitting in the wet leaves beside this lost soul.

"Don't we have to see if he's breathing?" I asked. "The heart can pump even if the lungs aren't working, right?"

"That means we'd have to roll him over," Joe said. We swallowed in unison and scrambled to our feet.

"Are we not supposed to disturb him? I mean, isn't this a crime scene?"

"But he's *alive*," Joe said. "You don't move a dead body. But what if he can't breathe, face-planted in the mud like this?"

So I peeled off my biking gloves, too. If I touched the man with them on, I'd have to throw them away. My hands, I could wash. I took the man's left hip, Joe took his left shoulder. We lifted and pushed.

Dead weight, I thought. That was a bad metaphor. In English class, Mrs. Rosen said that metaphors compare unlike things. Father-whoever-it-was was not unlike a dead thing. Not unlike at all. I couldn't believe I was thinking about metaphors when I was touching an almost-dead body for the first time in my life. But maybe that's how the mind works—distract yourself from horror so you don't freak out entirely.

His body was heavy and stuck. Pulling him loose made a sucking sound in the mud. When he flopped onto his back, I saw he was even bloodier in the front. Mud smeared his face. His nose was skewed at a crazy angle. A piece of broken tooth stuck in the mud and there was blood on his chest. But we could hear ragged breathing going in and out.

Below his chin, his white clerical collar was cloaked with mud and more blood. His crucifix had been wound around his neck. To choke him.

"Holy crap," Joe said under his breath. He untwisted the crucifix chain a couple turns to make sure it wasn't still cutting of the priest's air supply. Then Joe touched his own forehead, chest, and shoulder to shoulder. The sign of the cross.

I felt my breakfast rising for real, and I stumbled into the woods before it came sailing out, spraying the weeds with orange-juice-tinged oatmeal. When I was done, I wiped my mouth on my forearm. I didn't want to touch my face with the hand that had touched this half-dead man.

✖✖

Finally, finally the cops came. The rescue truck and the ambulance wailed up the hill to the LeHillier junk woods and wound down the dirt roads as close as they could get to us.

While the rescue squad loaded the priest onto the stretcher and put him in the ambulance, two detectives asked us ten million questions. Officer Mick was a little overweight with red hair. He fit the stereotype, like he got his share of donuts. Officer Kate had a kind smile, a no-nonsense brown ponytail, and looked like she could bench press a Pontiac.

"Where's Allie?" I asked.

"Who's Allie?" Officer Kate said, while Mick snapped pictures.

"Allison Baker. She called 911. From the gas station."

Officer Kate scribbled in her notebook. "Baker, huh?" She looked at Officer Mick and frowned.

We couldn't answer any of their other questions about Allie. "That's all we know," Joe said. "We ride with her every day, but we don't even have a phone number."

Officer Kate frowned. "You know where she lives?"

I shook my head. "I met her out riding on the trails, and we just meet at Scout's Last Chance every day to go for a ride."

Joe said, "Somebody has to know. She's won a bunch of mountain bike races."

The rescue truck and ambulance wailed their flashing lights back toward Mankato, bearing the almost-dead priest.

Officer Kate wrote some more notes, helped Officer Mick put the blue tarp in a big plastic bag, taped off the whole ravine with yellow plastic crime-scene ribbon like on TV, and took a bunch of pictures. Then they both scrounged around for other evidence.

Joe and I kept watching the rim of the hills for Allie. The only movement we saw was a mangy German Shepherd watching us from the treeline. When he saw us looking at him, he slunk off into the woods like a wolf.

Still, no trace of Allie.

SEVENTEEN

Alley Cats: Now You See Them; Now You Don't

July 2

The next day, the *Mankato Free Press* ran this story on the front page, with pictures of Joe and me:

Local Priest Left for Dead, Teens Credited with Saving His Life

A Mankato priest remains in a coma after a violent beating, and police say the Rev. Malcolm Dykstra would be dead if not for three teenagers who discovered his battered body while mountain biking Sunday morning.

Sadie Lester, 16, of Minnetonka, and Allison Baker, 16, of Mankato; along with Joe Montgomery, 17, of Phoenix, AZ, were riding bikes on trails along the Blue Earth River when Montgomery spotted what he

thought were feet under a discarded tarp.
When the teens looked closer and saw it was
a body, they called 911.

The Rev. Dykstra is a rector at St. John's
Catholic Church. He remains in critical
condition at Immanuel-St. Joseph's Hospi-
tal. Police are investigating, but they suspect
he was beaten and left in the woods during
Saturday night's storm.

"The kids are heroes," Officer Kate Ste-
vens said. "Their quick thinking saved his
life. There's no question—Father Malcolm
Dykstra wouldn't be alive if the kids hadn't
found him when they did."

Montgomery said, "The hill was all wet
and slippery. I fell and I slid right into the
ravine. Otherwise, we wouldn't have seen
him at all."

"We were scared to death," Lester said.
"When we first saw him, we thought he was
dead. Then Allie (Baker) recognized him
and we found a pulse. She took off to call an
ambulance."

Baker was not available for comment.

Det. Mike Rankin urged anyone with
information pertaining to the case to come
forward.

I wondered how Allie felt when she saw it.

I sent a copy of the paper to Mom and Dad in Egypt (but I only sent one so if they don't get back together, they will have to fight over it), and one each to Sara at Interlochen and Erica in Minnetonka, so she could read it whenever she got back from Europe. I squirreled away five extra copies without telling anyone. I've never been on the front page before.

Joe's picture made him look like a hoodlum. Reminded me of the first time I saw him, which is partly why I sent it to Erica and Sara.

✖✖

Still, no sign of Allie. Obviously the whole incident freaked her out, but we had no idea if it was the whole bloody scene or something about Father Malcolm. My guess was, it was the priest. At any rate, I was sure the *Free Press* article didn't help any.

Joe and I looked for her everywhere. No phone number, no idea where she lived. There was no *Baker* in the phone book with a LeHillier address. It was so strange to have spent a couple hours every day with someone and then, boom, have her drop off the face of the earth.

Joe and I rode up and down all the roads in LeHillier, all the residential streets (including Beaver Lane which made us laugh), past a house with no sign of electricity and an outhouse in back, and up and down the whole trailer court just in case we might see her or evidence of her. We got barked at by several hungry-looking dogs. I even called West High School to see if I could talk them into giving me her address or number, but of course, they wouldn't give out such information. I thought the counselor might be interested in a missing member of the student body, but the secretary won't let me get that far.

✖✖

Ever since my bike got soaked in the rain it didn't shift gears right, and Joe's front wheel needed to be trued, since he'd crashed. That gave us an excuse to go to the bike shop.

We went to A-1 Bike to ask Mike, the owner, if he knew how to find Allie.

A-1 was an old storefront shop in the oldest part of downtown Mankato. The door clanged open and the wooden floor creaked when we wheeled our bikes in. The ceiling was made of pressed metal tiles, and the place smelled of new bikes, old grease, and sweat.

Mike called to us from the shop counter, "Hey, I recognize you two from the paper. Friends of Allie. She told me about you." His grin lit the place up. "What can I do you local heroes for?"

Joe rolled his eyes. "We weren't heroes," he said. "It was all a stupid accident. If I hadn't crashed, we wouldn't have found the priest at all."

"Very few accidents in the world, my friend. Some things are meant to be." Mike was a big guy, not nearly as big as Scout or Thomas, but he was six feet tall and all muscle. His calves were chiseled and as big as Scout's biceps. He had a black flat-top haircut, and he didn't look like somebody you'd want as your enemy. Allie said he rode road bike, mountain bike, and BMX.

I didn't want to think about anything relating to Father Malcolm as *meant to be,* so I said, "Well, for one thing, my bike isn't shifting right."

"Your bike get wet or something?" Mike asked. "Might need new cables."

I told him about riding in the storm. "Speaking of the storm," I said, "we can't find Allie anywhere. Do you have a clue how we can find her?"

Mike's face turned ever-so-slightly red, and he gave us a funny, tight-lipped little smile like he was biting the inside of his cheek. He put my bike in the shop stand and whipped the old cables out of the cable housing. "Yup. Getting rusty in there. Look. We'll replace those for you. What makes you think *I'd* know how to find Allie?"

"Just, she has to register for races and stuff," Joe said. "We figured you have her address somewhere."

"We're getting pretty worried about her," I added.

"Funny you should ask." Mike dribbled oil into the cable housing. "When she started racing a couple years ago, she asked me if she could use the bike shop address on all her registrations instead of her home address." He threaded a new cable into the housing. "She picks up her race mail here. I guess she doesn't want anyone knowing where she lives." He shrugged. "Sorry." He dribbled another dab of oil into the housing and cut the new cable to the right length.

After replacing the other cable, Mike shifted my bike through the gears, turning the pedals while he did so. "Back wheel is out of true. Hang on while I adjust that." He slid the back wheel out of the dropouts and chain and set it in a truing stand.

"Looking forward to the race?" he asked.

Joe and I looked at each other.

"Allie told me you were both going to race. You are, right?"

"I'm scared," I said. "To death. Can't believe it's in two days. Might not do it if Allie doesn't show up."

Mike spun the wheel, stopped it, tightened a couple spokes with a spoke wrench, plucked the spokes like harp strings. "You'd better," he said. "She'd kill you if you didn't. She told me you guys are gonna rock." He plucked at more spokes and adjusted them. "Did you know Allie's seeded?"

"Seated? What's that mean?"

"*Seeded*. Allie's ranked. She's seeded first for the Expert race, but she's ranked third in the state. Overall."

Joe said, "You mean, of all Expert mountain bike women in Minnesota, Allie's ranked third?"

Mike nodded. "Yup." He was concentrating on the wheel.

"She never told us that," I said.

"Allie wouldn't," Mike said. "She's not exactly the bragging type." He lifted my wheel out of the stand and slid it back into position on my bike. "That should do it. So, that means if you've been chasing AllieCat all over the county and keeping up with her, you could do some serious damage at the Fourth of July race."

I felt a little prickle up and down my spine. What if I could do okay, or more than okay? It was too much to think about. "All I'm hoping," I said aloud, "is not to die of embarrassment."

"I just want to finish," Joe said.

Mike laughed. "This is for fun. Don't forget. Racing is *so much fun*. And I think you might surprise yourselves, if what Allie says is true." He lifted my wheel out of the stand. "You're good to go, Sadie."

I put it back on my bike. "Have you seen her?" I asked. "Allie?"

Mike lifted Joe's wheel into the truing stand. His face flushed and he shook his head. "Oh, no, that's not what I meant," he said, way too fast. "I mean, she's been telling me that all summer."

Joe and I looked at each other. I could tell Joe was thinking the same thing I was. We watched Mike work.

The front door dinged open and a guy with curly gray hair rode right into the store on a road bike. "Mikey! I think you need to come suffer with us today." He wheeled toward us, still balancing on his pedals.

Mike wiped his hands on his apron. "Meet Skarpohl. This is Sadie. Joe."

"I'd shake your hands," Skarpohl said, "but then I'd have to put my foot down. Nice to meet you. Mikey, you're ridin' today, aren't you?"

"Not today." Mike looked with longing at Skarpohl's road bike, which read *Skarpohl* on its slender yellow down-tube. "I want to. You know how much I love pain. But you know the deal. Business before pleasure." He spun Joe's wheel in the truing stand.

Then to Joe and me, Skarpohl said, "You should get road bikes. You could come suffer, too."

"Thanks," Joe said. "I think."

"Hey," Mike said without looking up from his work, "These two have been riding Allie Baker's wheel all summer. I think they know what suffering means."

"Oh ho!" Skarpohl laughed. "You know just what I'm talking about. Get yourself a road bike, girl. Then we can torture you, too."

I couldn't help but smile.

The crowd of roadies grew, and Mike introduced them all to us. TerryB, Grumpy Tom, Big Brian, Mini Brian, Mike's brother Matt, Danny, Ryo, and the "Tri-guys" who qualified for the Hawaii Ironman this year: Dan, Dave, and Doc. The bikes were a rainbow of colors and brands: Treks, Orbeas, Fujis, LeMond, Specialized. They looked light and fast.

"You two are good to go," Mike said, handing Joe his wheel.

While we paid Mike, Joe said, "So, you can't tell us where Allie is?"

"Mo-Jo!" Mike yelled.

A tall, skinny guy stuck his head out of the back room.

"I changed my mind," Mike said to Mo-Jo. He pulled his apron off over his head and hung it on a peg beside the workbench. "I've decided to go riding. Cover for me?"

Mo-Jo emerged fully from the back room. He reminded me of Shaggy from *Scooby-Doo*. He waved Mike away. "Have fun."

Then we rode away.

"You got the feeling I did, didn't you?" Joe asked.

"That Mike is avoiding telling us what he knows? Definitely."

"Notice he never said no, he hadn't seen Allie?"

❌❌

That night, I had a nightmare. I heard Allie screaming, "Run, Father Malcolm, run!" and I was screaming, "Run, Allie, run!" I woke up screaming just as a giant evil ATV had caught up to Allie. I was sweating. When I finally fell back asleep, I watched the crucifix on the chain getting tighter and tighter, and the mashed-up face turning bluer and bluer.

Scout shook me awake. "Sadie, Sadie, you're dreaming."

I opened my eyes.

"Pretty impressive lungs there, girl. You're *loud*. We can hear you screaming all over the house." He sat down heavily on the fold-out bed, testing it to make sure it would hold him.

"Nightmare, I guess. Father Malcolm. And Allie."

He brushed hair away from my sweaty face. "I s'pose every time you close your eyes, you see his smashed-up body."

I nodded. "Sorry I woke you up. I wish we knew where Allie is. That makes it all worse."

"She's got to show up soon."

"Scout—what if—what if whoever did this to the priest got to her? I mean, we know she made it to the gas station to call, but nothing after that. We've been assuming she took off—but what if—Scout, I'm scared."

He shook his head and brushed my hair back again. I expected the usual adult response of *don't worry, it'll be fine, I'm sure she's fine,* but instead Scout said, "I'm a little scared, too, Sadie. That's why I want you to be so careful. But after what I've seen, I'd feel sorry for anybody who tried to beat that girl up."

I smiled a little. "But still… I sure hope she's okay. And that she still does the race."

"I only know her a little bit, but it looks like she's pretty fearless. Seems pretty un-Allie-like not to race after all the training you guys have done."

We both sighed.

He stroked my hair once more and left me to stare at the ceiling in the dark. It took a long time to fall asleep again, so I lay there running my thumbnail over a cedar shake next to the roll-away bed. That way, I could smell the cedar. And not think about Father Malcolm's smashed-up face. And try not to worry about Allie. And try not to think about racing.

EIGHTEEN

Sister Mary Cecille

July 3

After Joe got off work the next day we took an easy spin around Mount Kato, not pushing for time, but reminding ourselves of the ruts, the turns, the twists in the climbs, the downhills.

"I have to do this," Joe said. "Otherwise, I know I'll freeze up during the race. I can't tell you how bad I want to throw up at the top of every big downhill."

"It's better than being a crappy climber," I said, standing in my pedals to crest one of the rollers. "Allie says if you can climb, you can race. The rest is bike handling."

"Yeah. That's why I'm nervous. Remember who crashed down the ravine?"

"You'll be fine."

We stopped at the bottom to rest. Joe said, "I heard you screaming last night."

"Sorry."

He shook his head and wouldn't look at me. "It's okay, Sadie. Sadie-Sadie. I don't blame you. I keep seeing the priest in my head, too—"

I tried to hide my smile. He'd given me a nickname.

"My bike sure handles better since Mike trued my wheel," Joe added. He started pedaling again and said, "Let's go see the nuns."

"Nuns? What nuns?" I stood on my pedals to catch up with him.

"There are nuns at every Catholic church, aren't there? Wouldn't somebody at Father Malcolm's church know Allie if she goes to church there or something? What the connection is?"

"I can't believe we haven't thought of that before."

The convent house matched the church, square and brick, with a red geranium on either side of the door. Very prim, very proper. When Joe rang the bell, a woman with short iron-gray hair, wearing black slacks and a white button-up shirt, came to the screen door with a smile. "Can I help you young folks?"

"Uh, hi." Joe smiled back. "We're looking for some—ah—any nuns—who know Father Malcolm—or have worked with him for a few years."

Her smile disappeared. "God bless him." She crossed herself. "That would be me. I'm Sister Mary Cecille." She pushed the screen door open.

"Nice to meet you," we chorused. "I'm Joe Montgomery." "I'm Sadie Lester."

Joe continued, "We're friends of Allie Baker. And she knows Father Malcolm."

Sister Mary Cecille stared at us. She glanced up and down the street and started to pull the screen door shut again. "Who sent you?"

"No one," I said. "We just need to find Allie."

"Please go away. We don't want any more trouble."

Joe and I looked at each other.

"We don't either," Joe said. "We just want to make sure Allie's okay. You know her, don't you?"

"Yes, of course I do. She went to CCD at our church, she was my student, and she—" She pursed her lips. "That's all I can tell you, really. One must respect the sacred confidentiality of confession. Now good day." She moved to close the screen door the rest of the way.

"Please." Joe reached out a hand toward her, stopping the door. "We can't find Allie. We're really worried."

"You should be," the nun said. "And be *careful.*" She looked up and down the street again. "It's probably not your business. Ask the Blessed Virgin for guidance. Maybe you shouldn't get involved. Be safe. Go home now." She tugged on the screen door. "Please." Joe let go. She shut the door and turned away.

"Sister Mary Cecille?" Joe wasn't giving up.

"Yes." Sister Mary Cecille stopped, without turning to look back at us.

"What if we'd gone home or just kept riding when we found Father Malcolm? What if we'd said it wasn't our business?"

She turned around and leaned toward the screen. "It was you." She looked from Joe's face to mine. "Oh, bless you. Thank you. For what you did. I wish I could help. But I can't. I really can't. And you may not be safe either. God bless you." She reached back and hooked the screen door, then floated away inside.

Chills traveled down my spine.

Back on the sidewalk, I turned to Joe. "What the hell?"

"You're swearing on holy ground."

"Yeah, but who the hell cares?"

"Well, it makes it worse, doesn't it?"

I looked to see if he was serious, and I realized he was.

"You really do take God seriously, don't you?"

Joe shrugged. "Yeah. But right now we gotta figure out what's going on. This just gets weirder and weirder. 'You should be? Maybe you shouldn't get involved? You may not be safe either?' Holy crap, Sadie."

"If Allie were here, she'd give *you* crap about saying that," I said. "Is religion why you never swear?"

"Not necessarily religion. God. God's name in vain and all that."

I looked at him, trying to figure him out. "You serious?"

He shrugged and nodded. "Think we should go talk to the cops again? See if they can help us put anything together?"

"Can't hurt, can it?" I knew that was the end of the God discussion.

We got back on our bikes, and Joe rode ahead of me.

At the police station, Officer Mick saw us and waved.

We asked for Officer Kate.

She hadn't seen Allie, she said. Officer Rankin saw us talking to Kate and came over to say hi. He was friendlier than he had been in LeHillier.

We told them about what Sister Mary Cecille said. "She's scared," I said, "and she wouldn't even let us in. Seemed terrified somebody would see us talking to her."

Kate and Rankin exchanged a look.

"You know something?" I asked.

"Nothing really. We want to find Allison Baker, too. If you see her, can you let us know?"

"I guess."

Officer Kate said, "If we find her, we won't be able tell you where she is, but we can let you know she's safe. And we'll tell her to contact you. Thanks for coming in."

When the door closed behind us, I said, "You're right. This summer *is* getting weirder and weirder. I thought it was going to be the most boring summer of my life. Sheesh. It's even weird to know so many cops."

Joe squeezed my hand. I wasn't sure anymore if what I felt was the thrill I always got when he touched me, or part of the overall shivers I had. We jumped back on our bikes.

✖✖

We'd gone about halfway to LeHillier, the long way around on County Road 66, when the roadies came up behind us and caught us, drafting in a paceline like geese in half a V. TerryB was "pulling" at the head of the line, and Skarpohl, riding next, patted Joe on the butt as they whirred past.

"See you two at the race," Mike yelled, and the whole line of them, colorful as tropical fish, skimmed away.

"Wow," Joe said.

"Ever thought about a road bike?" I asked.

"Not until this week."

✖✖

We cornered Scout at the Last Chance to tell him about Sister Mary Cecille. He poured us each a root beer and chewed his unlit cigar while he listened. "Joe?" he said. "Make sure you have your cell phone all the time when you guys are out riding."

Joe and I looked at each other and burst out laughing.

"And that's funny, why?"

We explained Allie's fetish about real mountain bikers not carrying cell phones.

Scout refilled our root beers. "Well, she's not here, is she? Listen, like I said before. Don't ride alone." He pointed a finger at each of us. "Either one of you. And stay out of the woods. Entirely."

We sat quietly for a few minutes. Joe and I both downed our root beers.

Joe said, "The last thing in the world I want to do is go look at Father Malcolm's beat-up body again, but..."

Scout and I both looked at him.

"But maybe we should go visit him."

"Are you nuts?" I said.

"Maybe. But I can't get the image of his bloody face out of my head, and maybe you'd quit having nightmares if we went to visit him. I mean, maybe, just maybe, the real thing isn't as bad as what we remember. He's still alive, after all. It might make him like a real live person instead of a nightmare. Ya think?"

The corners of Scout's mouth turned up slightly around his unlit cigar. He stood up and moved toward the bar. On the way, he patted Joe's shoulder. "Good man," is all Scout said.

NINETEEN
Life Support

July 3, continued

We took Joe's car to Immanuel-St. Joseph's Hospital. My first time in his car.

He opened the passenger door, and I was feeling flattered that he was being all gentlemanly, but actually, maybe he did it because he had to move two entire shoeboxes of CDs from the passenger side floor. He also had an iPod plug-in for his stereo, I noticed. There was a deodorizer in the shape of a trombone hanging from the rear-view mirror and emanating a strong pine scent, and an unopened pack of cigarettes under the dash.

He saw me eyeing the cigarettes as he slid into the driver's seat. "Unopened," he said. "They stay that way. When I can't smell cigarette smoke in here at all, I'll throw them out. Until then, it's like a test I have to pass."

I sniffed. "It's pretty faint already. More piney than anything."

He grinned, rolled his eyes, and started the car.

The hospital floor was smooth and shiny as fresh winter ice on a river. The place felt just about as cold as the river in winter, too.

Uncle Scout had called the hospital a couple times to check on Father Malcolm, but Joe and I had wanted to stay as far away from this place as possible. I didn't want to look at Father Malcolm's beat-up body and mashed-in face ever again. He had been unconscious for two days, since we'd found him in the ravine.

The information desk lady said, "Room 3411," as if a hospital visit was the most ordinary thing in the world. I suppose it was, to her.

Outside 3411, Joe and I stopped and stared at each other. We didn't have a clue how we were supposed to behave. He reached out and took my hand, sending a tremor through my body. We tiptoed in together.

Father Malcolm's broken nose was taped. A tube protruded from his neck, another tube ran into his arm below a cast, one went someplace under the bedcovers, and yet another tube piped yellow liquid from his lower regions. I tried not to look at that one. His eyes on either side of the white nose bandage were both blue-black sockets, from the broken nose or some other blow, I didn't know. I recognized a heart monitor and a respirator—I'd seen those on TV. He looked gray and scrawny, as if he were sleeping somewhere inside a tent of his own skin.

Barely louder than a whisper, we said, "Hi, Father Malcolm."

He said nothing. Of course. The only sound was his even, raspy breathing through the respirator. Heavy, like Darth Vader's breathing.

"Thought we'd come check on ya," Joe said.

Even breathing.

"We wanted to see how you are doing," I said, knowing how lame that sounded.

"I'm praying for you, Father," Joe said.

I jerked my head to look at Joe. "You are?"

"Yeah, aren't you?" he said.

"I…" I looked at the priest, and I whispered to Joe, "I guess I don't pray. But don't tell him that." I nodded toward Father Malcolm.

Even breathing. Being chicken and staying away from this place seemed more appealing by the second.

I said, "We wish you'd wake up. We can't find Allie. Allie Baker. And you know her, somehow. She wouldn't tell us exactly how. So I guess we need your help. To find her, I mean." I hadn't planned on saying all that, but it sort of spilled out. I could feel Joe's eyes on me. I remembered reading about suicidal people who stayed alive because they found out somebody needed them. Of course Father Malcolm wasn't suicidal, but this was about keeping him alive. "I wish you could wake up and help us find Allie."

Even breathing.

"Oh, yes. Everybody want him to wake up." The voice behind us made us jump. We dropped hands, whipped around, and an Asian nurse gave us a shiny white smile. "Everybody want the priest alive, yes. The police want him alive. Because as long as he is alive, he is not *murdered*. They want to know who did this to him."

Her smooth, olive-brown face, with dark eyes shining, was all business. She checked each monitor, his eyes, and his temperature in his ear as if taking care of potential murder victims was routine. "Yes, they wish for him to wake up." Her skin glistened; she was moving so fast, efficient fingers flying, stunning with her blue-black ponytail shining and her easy smile. She could make anybody want to be well. Her name tag said *Zia*. "The police, they want to hear what he has to say. So the police, they say, 'keep him alive, keep him alive.' Maybe he can tell police who did this thing to him."

We stared at her, and she asked, "Who, you think, would try to kill a *priest*? Such an *evil* person, to hurt a priest."

We shrugged. Joe nodded.

"My culture," she said, shaking her head, "in my culture, you *respect* the shaman. You *never, never* hit a shaman. What about this America? This *free* America? It confuses me."

"It confuses me, too," I said.

"Wait!" she cried. "You are the kids that save him. I know you. In the newspaper. You know, in my culture, when somebody's life is saved, you are responsible for the rest of your life." She lifted her eyebrows at us.

We stared.

"It's very good you are here talking with him. Yes." Still talking, she was moving out the door. "It's good, yes. Sit down." She pushed two chairs at us and we collapsed into them. "Keep talking. Maybe *you* can wake him up." And she was gone.

"Wait!" I said to the empty air.

Joe looked at me. "Did she mean *we* are responsible once we save his life? Or Father Malcolm is responsible now that we saved him?"

I shook my head. "No idea."

"No way am I gonna be responsible for Father Malcolm for the rest of his life," Joe said. "Just in case you wondered. Except I will pray for him."

I wanted to say to Joe that this guy was a priest, after all. He must have spent most of his life praying and look what good it did, but I said nothing. Joe could pray for him if he wanted to.

We sat there forever. We listened to the respirator wheezing air in and out of Father Malcolm's chest. We'd come to the hospital at 8:40 p.m. so we wouldn't have to stay long, as we would *have* to leave at nine when visiting hours were over. But it was only 8:48. Only eight minutes had passed, and neither of us could think of another single thing to say to try to bring Father Malcolm out of his unconsciousness. Nothing.

Breathing.

There was a whisper of sound in the hall. The nurse again, I expected. She came in silently last time. I turned to catch her on the uptake this time, but it wasn't the nurse.

It was Allie.

She slid around the corner of the door like an alley cat, silent and graceful. When she was riding her bike, her catlike movements flowed smooth as silk; that ability to land, tire-side down. The alley cat. On her feet, her AllieCatness seemed more unnatural, but I hadn't seen her walking around off her bike too many times, besides the night when she planted the cue ball in the Last Chance paneling. And I'd never seen her wearing anything but bike clothes.

Watching her grace in that moment, as she stepped through Father Malcolm's door in jeans and a tank top, I was aware again of how much I wished I *were* her, inside her perfect body with her fearless heart.

Here AllieCat was, flesh and blood, in the hospital room, face-to-face with us, and when she saw us, she got wild-eyed, as scared as the stealthiest alley cat surprised in the dark by a pit bull.

"Allie!" I cried.

She turned, her body one big reflex, and was out the door as quickly as she had come. As silently.

Joe and I were on our feet and out the door after her, with only a second's delay, but she was already way down the hall, strong, lean legs flying, spiked white hair bobbing, earrings flashing like rings of silver.

Smack! She ran smack, *smack*, into the beautiful Nurse Zia, who'd stepped out of another room at just the wrong moment. A tray of medicine flew through the air, and Zia, schmucked in the chest by 125 pounds of the leanest, fastest muscle around, went flying and landed on her butt on the hall floor, a multitude of colored pills bouncing around her. "Ugh!" she gasped.

"Stop her!" cried Joe.

The nurse made a one-handed grab for Allie's ankle, but her breath was knocked out and she wasn't as fast as Allie, who leapt over her and through a door to the stairway.

"Allie!" I screamed. "Stop! Please!" I jumped over Zia, too, shoved through the door, and thundered down the stairs. "Allie! Why—?" The door below me, to the front lobby and the outdoors, banged shut. I knew I'd never catch her, but I followed anyway.

I blasted through the lobby and out the front door. Allie had jumped on a junky bike, not her racing bike, and was halfway across the parking lot. "Allie!" I screamed. "Please come back! I just want to know where you've been … Allie!" I started across the parking lot toward her, but she powered away from me, deaf to me and the rest of the world.

I stood there for a half a second. Then I went back inside, trotted up the stairs, panting, to where Joe had stopped to help the beautiful nurse stagger to her feet and pick up the contents of the tray.

"This girl!" Zia fumed as I came around the corner. "This girl—"

"Come on, Joe, let's follow Allie," I said.

"You know this girl?" Nurse Zia asked.

"Yes," Joe said.

"Come on, Joe," I said, heading back toward the stairway. "Maybe we can catch her."

"This girl," Zia said, frowning at the contents of her tray, "she sneaks in here every night, at end of visiting hours."

"Every night?" Joe and I asked in unison.

"Yes, every night," said Zia. "Quiet as a cat, this girl. Slinks in here like the spirit of a cat. Like she weighs nothing at all. But now," she rubbed her chest, "I see she weighs something. Not a spirit after all. So you know this girl. Why, you think, she does this?"

"No idea. Sorry. Wish we knew."

"Joe, come on! We gotta follow her!"

"Sorry," Joe said again to Zia, and followed me back down the steps, two at a time.

Outside, we bolted to Joe's car, slammed the doors, and Joe backed out so fast he almost hit an old couple tottering from the hospital visitors' door toward their car. We squealed out of the parking lot and up the road, turned toward the big downhill on Marsh Street, but Allie, in her alleycat way, had disappeared.

The only living thing we could see was a stray German Shepherd–looking mutt loping down the sidewalk away from us.

"Least he looks like he knows where he's going," I said. "Wish we did."

"Sadie? That reminds me of the dog we saw in LeHillier, after we found the priest," Joe said. "Remember?"

I looked, but the dog had already disappeared over the hill.

TWENTY

Dead Ends

July 3, continued

Joe guided the car down the hill, but we knew that we were looking up and down side streets in vain. We drove around for twenty minutes without any hope of seeing her.

"I don't get," Joe said, tapping the steering wheel. "Why she'd run from *us*."

"Allie only mentioned Father Malcolm one time to me, and I could tell there was something she didn't want to talk about, but it didn't seem like a big deal. I don't get it, either. Why would she come see him every night, but run from us? What's the connection?"

Joe shrugged and drove back up the hill to a spot where we could look over the town. Lights twinkled across the valley and reflected on the river. Joe put the Grand Am into park and turned off the ignition. He squeezed my knee and left his hand on my leg.

"What now, Sadie-Sadie?" he asked. I liked it when he called me that.

I said, "We probably go home and get ready for the race tomorrow." I flopped my head back on the headrest. "Or we chicken out and don't race. Joe, I don't even know what I'm doing. I've never raced before. I don't want to do it without Allie there."

"No, Sadie-Sadie. You've got to race. This is what you've been training for. You've been working for this all summer, and you're gonna kick some butt in the Beginner class. You have to go ahead and do it."

"*We* have to," I corrected.

"Naw, I might chicken out."

I punched him lightly in the shoulder.

"Okay, okay." He grabbed my hand to stop a second punch. "We. And maybe, maybe, Allie will show up at the race."

"I sure hope so. And there's a $250 purse," I said. "I can't imagine her not showing up with a chance for a big win like that. Especially after what Mike said about her being seeded first."

"At least now we know she's okay. Physically, anyway," Joe said.

The sun had long since dropped over the edge of the world and the last of the dusky light was slipping away. From here, we could see the steeple of St. Peter's and Paul's Catholic Church, the one for the School Sisters of Notre Dame on Good Counsel Hill across another gorge, two Lutheran churches and a Methodist, but not Father Malcolm's Catholic church.

"So you really pray for him? Father Malcolm, I mean?"

"Yeah."

"I don't know if I believe in God or not," I said after a pause. "If I did, I'd pray. Did you mean it when you said that's why you never swear? Respect for God?"

He nodded.

"Do you believe it does any good—praying, I mean?"

"I'm sort of scared not to believe it. Since my brother died, especially. I'd rather pray into empty air and have it do nothing, than not pray if God really is listening."

"Isn't that what they call hedging your bets?" I asked.

"I guess. Sort of chicken-shit, isn't it?"

"Maybe." I shifted in my seat. "Or smart, maybe. Like fire insurance for eternity."

"Very funny."

"You've got a lot to lose if there *is* a God. And nothing to lose if there *isn't* one," I said.

"Except maybe a lot of energy and time," Joe said. "But a person can lose hope without God, don't you think? Wouldn't it make the universe sort of hopeless?"

"You mean, like hope for your brother ... to be somewhere besides just dead?"

Joe pulled his hand away.

I said, "But if you pray and pray and nothing happens, isn't that more hopeless than thinking we're on our own, and that we have to do everything we can for our own selves? Take charge of our own lives, instead of waiting for God to do something?"

Joe looked out his window, and I started to think I'd screwed up everything with him forever. Finally he looked back at me. "You're right, I guess. I can't stand the thought of John being *nowhere*. So I want to believe in God and all that. I have to."

"I'm sorry. I shouldn't have said that about John."

"It's okay."

I put my hand on his leg. I couldn't bring myself to tell him—and would never tell him—that I was sure his brother was dead. Just dead. Lights out.

I squeezed his knee and started to pull my hand back to my own lap, but he grabbed it and held my hand in both of his. "Sadie. I'm glad it was okay that we talked about him."

"Joe, he was your brother. Of course it's ... okay."

We sat without saying anything, holding hands, looking out over the hills, watching the city lights fighting off the darkness. "I forget what a beautiful city this is," I said.

"Easy to, with what we see every day," Joe muttered. "The trailer court in LeHillier is at the opposite end of this world." He slid one arm around my shoulder and pulled me closer. A thrill shot through my whole body. "Thanks, Sadie."

I nodded against his shoulder, my heart pounding, and I wondered if he could feel it.

"You're gonna kick butt in the race tomorrow," he told me.

I waited, feeling his fingers on my shoulder. His face was getting really close to mine in the near-dark, but he was studying my hand, which he was still holding, looking at my fingers, not my face. He said, "I think you'll surprise yourself." He let go of my hand and touched my cheek with his left fingertips. "In the race, I mean." He looked into my eyes and said, "Sadie-Sadie. I wish I knew what to do."

I held my breath, not sure what he meant, and not wanting to break the spell.

"We're not really cousins," he said.

"I know," I breathed. "I never worried about that, exactly."

He leaned his forehead against mine. "I'm glad. What are you scared about?"

I sucked in my breath, trying to figure out how to explain that I was afraid he liked Allie more than me, that I'd never really felt like this before, that without Allie, we weren't really whole, but I couldn't say all that.

And he said, "For the race, I mean?"

I had to concentrate, to remember the question and to answer. Nothing seemed to matter just now besides his arm around me, the nearness of his face, how his lips would feel. I forced myself to focus, and whispered, "Everything. I'm scared about everything. The downhills most, the downhill turns. How—how about you? You scared?"

He pulled back enough to look me in the eye. "I'm scared I'll freeze at the top and be too petrified to be able to go down."

I nodded, thinking about how I'd seen him do this. "You just go, Joe. Don't hesitate. Don't think. Just pretend it's you and me, following Allie." I grinned. "Ride through the chicken."

"What? The chicken?"

"Something Allie said to me. I said I was chicken to race. She said, 'Sadie, everybody's chicken. You just have to do it anyway. Ride through the chicken.'"

"Sounds like a butcher shop. A-1 Bike and Butcher."

We laughed.

Joe said, "What if Allie doesn't race? And we can't find her?"

I felt myself deflate a little. Joe was touching me, *touching me, holding me,* and talking about Allie. *Again.* Maybe he did really like her and just wouldn't admit it. Why, still, every time he touched me, did he have to talk about *her*? Or maybe she was our glue, and without her, there wasn't an us...not even a Joe-and-me *us.*

He ran his fingers up my left forearm. "Speaking of a butcher shop, you think seeing the priest beat up like raw meat just freaked her out? Some people can't handle blood. Maybe she took off because she was so freaked out."

"Allie?" I pulled back to stare at him. "You're kidding, right? She's tougher than that! Allie—*Allie* is *not* freaked out by blood, for chrissake."

"How do you know? Maybe it's the one thing in the world she's a wuss about. There has to be something."

"Allie? A wuss? You kidding? She sewed up her own leg one time when her chainring cut her open and she needed stitches and didn't have health insurance, for cryin' out loud. I don't think that much of anything freaks Allie out. She has more guts than y—"

Joe pulled his arm away, and I realized too late what I was about to say. "I'm sorry. I didn't mean *that*. I just meant that nothing freaks her out. I know it wasn't just…the…blood." But my words were lame and I lost steam while I tried to backpedal.

"Well, sorry!" Joe turned and put both hands on the steering wheel. "Sorry I'm more of a wuss than Allie."

"Joe, you're not—" I reached out, touched his arm, but he shrugged me off and stared out across the river valley.

"I'm sorry," I said again, but he didn't respond.

Finally he said, "So if she wasn't freaked out, why did she take off?"

"I didn't say she wasn't freaked out, Joe. Just that it wasn't the blood. Something else freaked her out."

"What, then?"

"If I knew that, we wouldn't be doing this, would we?"

"Oh, wouldn't we?" Joe sighed heavily and turned on the ignition. "I was hoping you and I would be doing this anyway."

"Wait. Joe. Yes! I was hoping that too. That's not what I mean! I can't say anything right." I wanted his arm back, wanted the moment back, wanted more than anything to take back my words, to have his face close to mine.

But he guided the car toward home and I sank against the passenger door.

TWENTY-ONE

Night

July 3, continued

When we walked in the door, Aunt Susan handed me the phone. "Your dad."

Joe kept on walking and went straight to his sanctum in Scout's office.

"Hi Dad," I said, watching Joe disappear.

"Hi Honey. Happy Fourth of July! You ready for your big race?"

"Mostly terrified."

"That's good," he said. "If you weren't scared, you wouldn't respect what you're doing. Being scared is good, Sadie. Good luck."

I talked to Mom, too, and I wanted to tell them in the worst way about all the insanity of Father Malcolm and the nuns and the detectives, but Timmy wouldn't leave the room, and Aunt Susan was listening, and I couldn't say I'd take the phone in the study because Joe was in there, so I asked about Nefertiti and then said good night.

And I went downstairs and shut myself in CCC.

I'd changed into pajamas, and crawled into bed with a book, when there was a knock at the closet door.

"Yeah?"

Joe stuck his head in. "Can I come in?" He looked sad, really sad.

"Sure." I sat up, pulling the sheet up to my armpits because I was only wearing my oldest, comfiest, see-through T-shirt.

"Can we talk?"

I nodded, patted the bed beside me for him to sit down. He did.

"I can't stand feeling like this. I know I'm a wuss, but I don't want to be. I lost John. I don't want to lose you—"

I let go of the sheet with one hand and grabbed his hand. "Joe, I'm really sorry for what I said. That's not what I meant. I just meant that I'm sure Allie didn't disappear 'cause of being freaked out by blood. Besides, she's got way more guts than me. No comparison. And sometimes I wish I *were* her. And she's got enough guts that she's been at the hospital every night. I'm so sorry." The words tumbled out. "Sometimes I don't think what I'm saying. I didn't mean—"

But his finger was on my lips and he was smiling into my eyes. "It's okay. I know I can be a wuss. It just drives me crazy that I think you like Allie more than me, or that she's more important to you than I am, and that you admire her more. And I guess I'm jealous, so I came to apologize."

"You are? I mean, it does? I mean, no, I don't like her more. Joe, I like—"

His finger was back on my lips. "You don't have to explain. But thanks. I had to say that 'cause we need each other right now. The race, Allie, Father Malcolm—this is crazy enough without being mad at each other."

I nodded, too vigorously. I bit my lip and plunged in. "Joe, I get jealous because it seems like you always bring Allie up whenever we're close. Like every time you touch me, you have to bring up her name."

"Ha. You serious? I thought it was you who always did that."

Our eyes met, and we smiled.

"'Night, Sadie."

"'Night, Joe."

My heart was so much lighter. I only wished he'd leaned over and kissed me.

TWENTY-TWO

Race Morning

July 4

Fourth of July morning. I didn't have to work because I'd taken the day off for the bike race. I woke up, saw 5:30 on the clock, and turned over. The race wasn't until nine. For once I could sleep in.

The next thing I knew, Joe was in my closet-turned-bedroom. "Sadie."

Joe looked awful. Worse than last night. His eyes drooped like he hadn't slept at all.

"Joe, what's wrong?" I sat up. "What time is it?"

"Six thirty."

I was aware again of wearing only my thin T-shirt, the closeness of the closet.

He sat on the edge of my roll-away. He wasn't looking at my thin T-shirt or what he could probably see beneath it. "Go for a walk?" he said quietly. "We'll wake somebody up if we talk here."

"Okay." I pulled a sweatshirt over my T-shirt, flannel pants over my boxers, and stepped into my flip-flops.

We shushed Peapod, let him out the door with us, and walked down the road toward the waste treatment plant, through the Dumpster cemetery but avoiding the woods. Peapod bounded around behind us, then in front of us, delighted we were walking, delighted for the dewy grass to roll in and for morning smells to sniff.

We passed the north end of the trailer court and the junked mobile homes where I'd met Allie. In the early morning, barely there light, we eyed the trailer on its side, without a floor, its pipes hanging out like intestines, and we both shuddered. Joe took my hand. We walked, holding hands, until we reached one of the Blue Earth River overlooks.

Joe dropped my hand and climbed onto a rock, looking down at the river. I followed him. The water rippled in all the same places that it always did.

"It's going to be a hot day to race," I said. The valley was an explosion of five hundred shades of green, surrounding the black river water and reflected in it. The change in temperature overnight made mist rise in thin wisps that hovered like ghosts over the shimmering water.

Joe stared into the still-life photograph before us. Then, as if he was pained, he sat down, curled up tight, in the fetal position, hanging onto his knees as if they might shoot out and down the bluff if he didn't hold on. "I didn't think I'd ever be able to sit on a cliff again," he said finally.

I watched his face and waited for him to explain. I sat down as close to him as I dared.

Peapod sensed Joe's mood, jumped up beside him on the rock, and nosed his big head into Joe's lap. His big yellow head rested on Joe's thigh and Joe rubbed one golden ear.

"It doesn't break your heart. It's bigger than that."

"Joe. Tell me what you're talking about."

He went on. "When you scream, the noise isn't big enough. You scream from the inside, but it splits you open like an egg. I felt cracked wide open like a broken egg, and I was screaming on the path at the Grand Canyon, like all that was left of me was a broken shell, and I couldn't scream loud enough."

I stared at him. I knew my mouth was hanging open. I could tell that Joe had been thinking these words for a long time, holding them in. He dragged his eyes from the river far below to look at me. I put my hand on his knee. "Go on."

"My brother," he said. Peapod pulled his head back, cocked his head, and whimpered, watching Joe's face.

I waited.

"When John died. But you know all that, right, Sadie?"

I shook my head. "All I know is you're here 'cause your brother got killed in some horrible accident hiking and you needed to get away. Aunt Susan won't talk about it, and I asked Uncle Scout to tell me, but he said you probably needed to tell me yourself. That's all he'd say."

"You never asked me."

"You kidding? I wanted to ask so bad. I figured you'd tell me if you wanted to."

"So, here goes then, Sadie-Sadie. My brother John and I were hiking along the edge of the Grand Canyon. We loved going there. My twin brother and me."

I tried not to move. "Twins," I said, barely more than a whisper.

"He fuckin' *fell*, Sadie. I...I watched him splat on the rocks. Four *hundred* feet. Splat. Like he exploded."

I stared. My mouth felt like sand.

"He was being stupid. *Stupid.* He was jumping around, showing off on the ledges to piss me off 'cause he knew I'm scared of heights, so he kept jumping around and he kept saying over and over—'precipices, Joe, precipices!' And he jumped back a little too far and slipped right off, me five feet away, watching him go, listening to him scream...and I started to scream..."

I wasn't sure if this was real, or a bad dream that had started in the hospital room, or on the road with the rednecks, or when we found Father Malcolm, or when Joe suggested Allie was gay, or maybe back when the cannonball explosion landed me here in LeHillier. The whole world as I used to know it had shifted, and I grabbed at the rock on each side of me. I had to hang on or I might go flying off, but the rock was smooth and there was nothing to hang onto.

"Oh, Joe," I heard myself say.

"They sent me up here, Sadie. Minnesota's about as far away from the Grand Canyon as you can get. So they sent me here." He looked at me, so much pain in his eyes it hurt to look at them. "So that's my story. He was my twin, so it's like I splatted down there, too. At least half of me did. That's why I totally freak at the top of the big hills. I'd always freaked out a little, but now...now sometimes I just freeze, and all I can think about is watching him go...and it's like I have to push myself over, 'cause I can't go on purpose. John—he was fearless on the mountain bike, like Allie. I thought I *had* to do this, to keep mountain biking, to get over this, to face it, to ride the big hills, but it's not getting any better. And then I fell and flew over the ravine...and that was bad enough, but then I almost landed on top of Father Malcolm. And that freaked me out more than falling. And—and I'm scared to not pray. Because I didn't pray that day. The day John fell. Until it was too late. And I don't want John to be nothing. I want to believe he's still alive somewhere."

"Oh my God," I said.

"Holy crap," Joe said, leaning back, the palms of his hands behind him on the rock. Peapod shifted, too. "Fuck and shit."

"Joe," I said, "you are using profanity."

He swiped at his eye with the back of his hand. "Sure as fuck am." Then he yelled over the river valley, "Doesn't fuckin' matter, does it?" He threw his head back, looked into the sky. "Wish I had a smoke. Damn. I really want a fucking cigarette."

"No you don't," I managed to say. I was in slow motion, watching myself from the outside. I reached out and put my arm around his shoulder and lay my head against his neck. I felt tears dripping from my face onto his shoulder. I hadn't even noticed I was crying, but I didn't stop them. I wrapped the other arm around him, too. Joe sat there while I cried, and after a while, his arms wrapped around me, too, and I felt teardrops plunking on my temple from his face. And then he started sobbing. And I held on tight.

We sat like that for what felt like a long, long time. The sun reflected on the river as it slid up over the hill, almost where the cannonball had disappeared over a month ago. When the sun launched off the horizon into its arc for the day, the rays heated us up instantly.

I let go and wiped snot and tears from my face. Joe did the biker blow, holding one nostril shut and blasting the snot from the other nostril. He sniffed.

Then he looked me in the face. "Guess that means I trust you. Nobody else knows all that. And I sure haven't cried with anybody else."

I tried to smile, but it was a lame attempt. The ends of my mouth sort of curled up in a sad sort of way, and that was all I could muster.

"Thank you." He brushed my cheek with his knuckles. "That's why I'm such a chicken shit. Talk about needing to ride through the chicken. So if you didn't admire me as much as Allie before, now you can write me off entirely as a crybaby who's scared of the hills—"

"Joe! Stop it—"

"It's true, Sadie. But I had to tell you this crap. I needed you to know. I'm the one who should have fallen. Not John."

"No, you shouldn't, Joe. Last night, when I told my dad how scared I am, he said, 'If you weren't scared, you wouldn't respect what you're doing. Being scared is good.' That's my dad, the archeologist. John didn't respect the Grand Canyon, Joe. The only reason he died was because he didn't respect the danger. You respected it. It kept you safe. You respect Mount Kato. So you can do it. Fear is good."

Joe bit his lip. "Your dad sounds cool," he whispered.

"He is," I said. We were quiet for a minute. "So..." This time I took Joe's hand. "So, Joe."

"Yeah?" He looked at me and sniffed.

"Why did you need to tell me? I mean, why *me*?"

"Don't you know, Sadie?"

I shook my head.

"'Cause I like you. Lots. I need you to know. If you're going to like me back, you have to know all of it." He looked away, over the river. "I don't care so much if you think I'm sort of a wuss if you understand why."

"Joe."

"Hmm?"

"I think you're brave. And wise. And Joe? I like you. Okay?"

And he turned back to me. "You sure?"

I nodded. And this time I could smile for real.

And we leaned toward each other and I was finally, finally going to get to kiss him, to feel those lips. And Peapod barked.

We jerked back. Peapod growled. He leaned against Joe and his hackles stood straight up.

"What, Peapod?" I whispered. "Joe, the only time I've heard him growl—"

"I know. Shhh." We stared into the edge of the woods. Nothing that we could see. Peapod sat down, still staring. His growl crescendoed, and then finally he relaxed and wagged and licked Joe's face.

Joe took my hand and Peapod's collar. "That's creepy. Come on, Sadie. Peapod, come!" We turned and walked toward Scout's. When we passed the trailer cemetery, we ran. We raced Peapod back to Uncle Scout's. Peapod beat us both, but Joe was ahead of me by only two steps when we got to the garage, breathless.

TWENTY-THREE

Race Day

July 4, continued

My stomach was all fluttery from being so close to kissing Joe and from whatever scared Peapod. The real fear hit only when we started to get ready. Race day.

"Thanks for talking to me," I said to Joe as we loaded up backpacks. We had too much stuff to carry it just in our jersey pockets.

"I had to. Thanks for listening."

"So how you doing? About the race, I mean."

"I think I'm going to throw up. That's how," Joe said. He ran his thumb along the inside of a brand-new inner tube that he was bringing for a second spare, before he folded it and put it in the backpack.

I felt selfish to be glad I wasn't the only one on the verge of vomiting.

Besides extra inner tubes, we brought money, extra water bottles, Gatorade, granola bars, and GU—which is high-energy fuel that you can squeeze out of a packet into your mouth during a hard ride. We also crammed in flip-flops to wear after our races; mountain biking shoes with cleats underneath aren't the best walking shoes, and we wanted to walk around to watch the other races.

We pulled into Mount Kato at 7:55. The Beginner class was first, at 9:00, for people like me; then Sport for "competitive experienced riders of average ability," including Joe; then Comp for "competitors looking for state or regional recognition"; then Expert/Elite, and the riders who'd done so well in Comp or Sport that they had to move up. Nobody who had a racing license and experience racing could ride Beginner. I scanned the crowd for a head of spiky white hair, but I didn't see Allie.

At the registration tent, we got our numbers, paid our fees, and got our free water bottles. We attached our race numbers to the front of our handlebars, and Joe asked me if I wanted to do a warm-up lap.

I looked at him like he was nuts. "I have to ride two laps as it is. Shouldn't I save my energy for the race? I'm pretty warm from just riding over here."

"I'd do a small hill or two if I were you," he said. "Just to get the blood flowing good. Get the lactic acid out of your muscles if you can. You're a good climber, and you could be kickin' some butt on the hills. Think about how much better you ride hills when you're warmed up. Just let your body ride. Don't think too much. Ride like you always do. Pretend you're chasing Allie. Remember, this is supposed to be fun."

"Yeah, take your own advice."

The race course at Mount Kato started on the flat grass at the bottom of the ski hill. The single track zig-zagged up the hill, which seemed like a mountain from the bottom. At the top, it leveled off and wound around some ponds and up and down, then around in the woods on the top and back of the hill. There were three levels of trails, from "easy" to "technical," and the race used the technical trail whenever possible. I was mostly scared about the descent. It was a long bumpy grind, with switchback curves that could send you flying into the woods. Thank goodness, the Beginner race used the "Mad Squirrel" downhill. The rest of the races used a hill called (for obvious reasons) "the Luge."

I rode around some more, but I didn't want to do a whole lap. At least pedaling kept my legs from shaking.

Finally, it was time for the Beginner class to line up. I looked around. A handful of people my age, three men, one middle-aged woman, and lots of eleven and twelve-year-olds. About forty people in all, I'd guess. We all looked shaky. I caught Joe's eye on the sideline, and he shrugged and grinned. "Good luck, Sadie-Sadie," he called. "You can take this. Just ride smart on the downhill. You'll be strong on the climbs."

I thought about wishing the girl next to me "good luck," but I couldn't quite look at her. I wanted to win, and I really didn't want good luck for her. There wasn't room for the best luck for both of us, so I didn't say anything. I pretended to adjust my glove, feathered my brake levers, and the gun went off.

It was a madhouse. Bikes weaving side-to-side as the kids stood to get a sprint toward the big hill. I was instantly behind about a dozen teenagers and older kids and two of the men. The flat turned into single track, and I swerved off the trail onto the grass and rode around three of the kids right away. Then I was back on the track. I dodged onto the grass, around a couple more.

I looked up and counted nine bikes ahead of me, so I was tenth going up the hill. I stayed right there, pacing myself behind the boy wearing a Salsa jersey and a silver helmet. He was riding a Gary Fisher bike that looked like it cost a fortune. He stood into the climb. It was early for that unless he was a really strong standing climber. I stayed seated, spinning in an easy gear, feeling the burn already in my quads, but knowing it would get worse before it got better. The kid was falling back from the wheel in front of him, so on the next switchback, I curved outside him and passed, sliding back into the singletrack in front of him.

"Sonofabitch," I heard him spit out, between heavy breaths.

My breath was heavy, too, but I concentrated on making it even, not ragged. In, out, in, out. Slow and deep instead of fast and hyper. Like the bass drumbeat for the faster pedal cadence.

I kept my rhythm, trying to ride my own pace, and I pedaled past a couple more riders. Now I'd moved into seventh position, but that didn't mean anything yet. We were barely started. I hung where I was, trying to keep my rhythm, until we were two switchbacks from the top. Then I pulled onto the grass, shifted, and accelerated uphill, standing, pumping like Allie had shown me, past three more bikes including one of the men. He saw me and stood to match me, but his legs were shot and he couldn't keep up. Two boys who looked about my age and one man were in front of me. All the eleven-year-olds were behind me now. I slid back into line to crest the top of the hill.

The guys ahead of me seemed fairly strong, so I was happy to follow them. If they started to break up and one of them went out ahead, I would try to pass and follow the leader. But for now, they stuck close together, swooping through the hairpins one after another, rattling over the corduroy roots, sifting through the soft dirt. I tried to let go of thinking, let my bike flow, pretend I was following Allie. Sometimes it worked, but sometimes I started to think, "I'm racing, I'm doing this, and I'm doing okay!" and then a gap seemed to open up between me and the bike ahead of me, so I shut off my brain and thought about the wheel ahead of me and the terrain. Nothing else. Legs pushing, loose arms, balance. *Breathe in rhythm. Flow.*

I got the familiar buzz in my arms. The rattling and vibration shook all my muscles and bones so much, my arms hummed with it. We charged toward the big downhill. My heart was in my throat. I'd ridden this over and over with Allie and with Joe, but this time, I was terrified. I looked over my shoulder to see if anyone was on my wheel. I couldn't see anybody beyond the curve in the trees. The four of us seemed to have broken away off the front.

That quick turn of my head cost me a bread-loaf-sized rock. I saw it too late, and my front wheel made a direct hit.

I flew over my handlebars. Grass rushed toward me, and I slammed into the weeds, face and shoulder down, too late to tuck and roll. "Oof." I couldn't get my breath for a second, but when I did, I jumped up. My shoulder hurt but my arm moved just fine, so I was okay. I tried to catch my breath, spit dirt, and pull my bike back into position. The threesome were zipping away from me toward the bottom of the hill, and I'd just made a stupid, stupid move.

I jumped back on. I could hear more bikes in the woods behind me, so they were closing in. I wanted to go down the hill without an audience. Back on the bike, I clipped into my pedals and looked down. It looked too long, too steep, not possible. How had I ever done this? I felt that pull over the edge, like looking down from any great height gave me, and I felt Joe watching his brother fall and splat on the rocks below, and I froze. I fell on a stupid rock. How could I do this giant hill ... ? I couldn't.

But inertia and gravity moved me, even without pedaling, over the lip of the descent, and I was going down. Too late now. *Can't think about Joe. Watch the terrain. Miss that rut, follow that line. Don't think. Ride.* I feathered my back brake, didn't touch my front brakes. That would be sudden and certain death. Well, certain crash, probably not death. *Don't think about death. Ride.*

A kid from behind came shooting past me on the downhill, another one on his wheel. Way too fast, reckless, fearless, thinking this was their chance to make a big move. The first one wasn't using brakes at all. Stupid, unless he was truly an expert, which he couldn't be. Then he hit a rut and a root in succession, and he was airborne, shooting sideways right into my line of descent. I turned my handlebars in the direction he was falling from, so I'd go behind his bike as he moved away from me.

The kid behind him hit him, and landed in the rocks. I hit the second kid's back tire in the trail but I rode over it as if it were a rock or root; I was airborne for a moment and just kept going. I heard more riders coming around the bend and down, and the crashing and thrashing behind me told me there was a huge pile-up on top of that kid on the slope. I was lucky, in spite of my stupid fall.

I made it to the bottom. My hands were soaked with sweat. If I didn't have gloves on, I wouldn't have been able to hang on to my handlebars. I exhaled. I'd made it down. One down.

Breathe, breathe. Ride. I swooped down the remaining grassy slope, hit the rise and caught air, landed safely on cocked legs, and blasted across the flat. The crowd was cheering. For me! Joe was next to the single track, screaming,

"Sadie! You're great! You're in fourth! Just ride. You're doing great!"

I kept breathing, trying to relax. I couldn't relax. I hit the bottom of the switchback uphill and started it all over. This time, I was shaking from the downhill, the fall, and the near miss with the kid down, and I was on the tired side of the adrenaline rush. It had pumped through me and was gone. My legs felt like lead, and my lungs felt like deflated balloons.

The threesome was only about forty feet ahead of me on the switchback, but I was slow. My bike and I seemed to weigh five hundred pounds. I thought of Allie in front of me, of following her, and I pushed, trying to catch her instead of those three racers, but nothing felt better, nothing worked, and I was just slow. Nobody caught me on the uphill only because it had taken everybody else so long to untangle from the pile-up on the descent. I made it up the hill with lead in my legs, a long way back from the leaders.

"Sadie! Breathe! You're doing great!" Joe screamed up the hill after me. I headed for the back stretch into the woods.

I kept spinning my legs at a high cadence to get my breath back and get rid of the lead, that lactic acid. Then, as fast as it came, the lead was gone. I'd recovered from the climb. I stood up and sprang over the hilltop. Round the first corner, then another, a swoop around, and bam, I was on the back of the threesome again.

We wove through the obstacles for the second time, in almost the same order. There was another sloping uphill after the pond, and this time, I felt strong, so I powered off the track and around the kid in back. He swore under his breath, but he couldn't re-pass me. He was breathing like a freight train and riding out of his league already.

We came into a straightaway through thick trees, and there were a few spectators in the meadow, clapping, cheering.

"Sadie!" I heard. A familiar voice. Allie! *Allie!* "Sadie, you're kicking some serious butt!" Allie screamed. "Just ride. Relax. Breathe!" Her white head was a blur beside me, but I could see her smile and her head-jewelry flashing in the sun. Her eyebrow ring caught a sparkle. "Go, girl! You're awesome. Just ride. Loose arms on the bumps. Relax!" And I was past her. She yelled after me, "You're doin' it! You're ridin' through the chicken!"

I was smiling in spite of the burn in my legs and lungs. *Allie is here. I can do this.*

Next corner, next rise, a small clearing, and I saw an open spot. I jumped forward into a tiny gap and swerved off the trail and passed one more bike. I was in second! The single track through the rest of the woods would keep us in this order until the descent.

We approached the big hill down, and I watched for rocks this time, my eyes on the terrain. Over the top, and my heart froze—sweat sprung to my ribs, my hands, but I tried to just let the bike flow. Fifty feet down, the kid

I'd passed last came sailing by me and then slowed just enough to fall in line in front of me. The bumps and ruts rattled us, but we hung on to the smooth descent in the grass. I bent low over my handlebars, cranking with everything I had left in my legs, which was mostly jelly and all pain, but I stuck. We flew over the last jump like a school of salmon leaping upstream. I was coming into the finish line in third place. I cranked on my pedals with all I had left.

I hit the line, and the crowd was going nuts. Joe grabbed me before I even came to a stop, and we almost toppled over on my bike.

"You did it! You did it! You got third!"

The judge wrote down my number, and Joe and I moved off the course. The Sport class was getting ready, but it would be a good thirty or forty minutes before all the Beginners were done. I couldn't believe I'd done it. I held up my shaking hands and Joe laughed.

Only then did I see that my shoulder was bleeding, and my jersey was ripped. There was dirt in my helmet, and my whole right side was streaked with grass and dirt, and I was missing a little skin on my elbow and above my knee. But none of that mattered.

"You crashed?" he asked.

"Yup. And it's not the end of the world. We can survive a crash. We've both proved that now."

He threw his arms around me again. "I'm so proud of you."

"Joe, Allie's here. Up in the woods."

"Yeah? Dressed to race?"

I nodded.

"All right!" he said.

Joe rode around to stay warm while he watched more finishers come in.

I went to park my bike. I took off my helmet, peeled off my shoes and filthy socks, put on my flip-flops, and took a fresh Gatorade bottle. After finding a paper towel, I dumped some water on it and wiped off my wounds. Nothing was too bad. The shoulder might need a big Band-Aid, but no stitches. It was part of the deal. I took the Gatorade and sat in the shade of the Mount Kato Chalet and Ski Shop, basking in the after-adrenaline of a good race.

A mountain bike rolled over to me. I saw the shaved legs of a roadie and moved my eyes upward to see curly gray hair. Skarpohl. "Good for you," he said. "I bet they won't let you ride beginner again." He grinned at me, a twinkle that lit up his whole weathered face. "You know, if you don't fall down, you can't say you've ridden a mountain bike."

I laughed. "I like that philosophy. Are you racing today?" I nodded at his mountain bike.

"Yeah. Gotta be stupid a few times a year. Anyway, good race," he said. "You need to buy a road bike."

"Thanks," I said, and he was gone.

Joe spun over. "Would you take a couple bottles to the top of the hill for me? Up at the feed zone? I might need one on each lap. Maybe some GU, too. I'll carry a couple, but just in case?"

So I emptied out the backpack and reloaded it with our extra water bottles and GU, left the rest under my bike, and gave Joe a good-luck hug, thinking about how much physical contact we'd had today. I started up the hill. The "feed zone" was a designated open place on the flat ridge on top, out of the woods, where people could stand with extra bottles or even food in case one of the racers started to "bonk." Bonking meant running out of energy—glycogen stores are gone, zip, zilch, and you can hardly see straight or turn your pedals when it happens. If you get some carbs into your system, you can actually keep riding.

The Beginner race had only taken me an hour and twenty minutes, not long enough to need extra water bottles, but I was sure some of the Beginning racers still out there were hoping for a new bottle by now. Joe's Sport race went for three laps. The Expert women's race was four laps, and Expert men's was five. Halfway up, I turned and watched the Sport class starting to gather by the starting line. I waved at Joe. He waved back.

I headed for the part of the woods where I'd seen Allie. It was only about a hundred meters from the "feed zone," so I had lots of time to try to find her before Joe came through.

Lots of people were climbing up the hill here, some with coolers, some with picnic baskets. There were still beginners riding the ridge. Lots of time difference between the winners and the kids at the back.

"You're doing this!" I yelled at a girl of about ten. "Good job!" She gave me a big smile and stood on her pedals to go faster. I clapped.

I looked and looked for Allie. No sign of her. Finally, the starting gun went off for the Sport class. I gave up and headed for the feed zone to cheer for Joe.

I settled into a grassy spot to wait when I heard, "Sadie. Hey."

I whirled around. "Allie!"

She grinned at me from the treeline, came over and squatted on the grass beside me. "Great job. You rocked."

"I'm so glad you're here," I said. "*Where* have you been!? Why'd you ditch us at the hospital?"

"Listen," she said quietly. "I'm taking off *right* after my race. I can't stick around a minute for awards or prizes, and I intend to *win* today. At least I hope I can."

I nodded. "Yeah?"

"Will you get my prize money, if I win any, for me? Bring it to the back door of A-1 at four o'clock this afternoon. Okay?"

"The bike shop? There's a back door?"

"Yeah. Go down the alley and come up the rickety-looking wooden steps beside the big A-1 painted on the wall. Then inside, there's a hallway. It's the door straight ahead."

"They're not open on the Fourth of July."

"No, but I'll be there. Bring your bike inside. Don't leave it outside so anybody will see it—or rip it off. Four o'clock. On the dot. Can you do it?"

I thought about the picnic my family was planning for the time between the parade at noon and the concert in the evening. Thomas's family was coming; our whole group hadn't been together at Scout's since Memorial Day. I hoped I could sneak away at four p.m. I'd have to. I had to do this for Allie. I nodded.

"Will they give it to me? Your prize money?" I asked.

"I'll tell Mike. You know, Mike from A-1. He'll give it to you. I'll give you my race number at the finish line, too, to take with you. That is, if I win something. I have to leave the second I'm done racing. So meet me at the finish line to get my number, and come to A-1 at four o'clock. Okay?"

I nodded again. "Allie, what's going on? Where have you been? Why do you have to split?"

"I'll tell ya later, at the bike shop" she said. "Not now. Got it?"

"Okay, I guess."

"I gotta go warm up. And you need to cheer for Joe. See you at four. On the dot. Promise?"

"Of course."

"See ya," she said.

"Allie. Good luck."

"Thanks. Sadie, you were *awesome* today. I knew you'd do it. You killed that chicken."

I grinned. "Thanks, AllieCat. You go kick butt now."
And I turned back to watch the race and wait for Joe.

✖✖

In the third lap, Joe struggled, but he rode really well.
He threw an empty bottle toward my feet—which landed
within fifteen feet of me—and grabbed the fresh one I was
holding out. "You're doin' it!" I said, just like Allie had said
to me. "You're ridin' through the chicken." He grinned in
spite of himself.

He came in seventeenth. The Sport class was tough.
Ryo, the roadie, got first, and Mike's brother Matt got second. Since there were almost sixty riders in his race, Joe
wasn't disappointed with seventeenth. He was happy. "If
I'd stopped smoking a month earlier, I probably would
have placed in the money," he said. "Next time."

"I think you did great," I said. "How'd you do at the
top of the Luge?"

"I just kept riding," he said. "I thought about you, actually, and I just kept going." He smiled. We brought the last
of our extra bottles uphill to cheer Allie from the woods.
The sun blazed down. The dirt trail and the grass all radi-
ated heat. It was good to be able to wait in the shade.

Allie looked like a pro. There were only twelve women
and girls in her Expert race. Joe and I stood in the clearing
at the top of the hill to watch the gun go off. Allie rode to
the front on the first flat before the uphill. The cluster was
together at the hill, but by the time they were halfway up,

the twelve of them had spread out. Allie was a ferocious climber. I realized, watching her, how much I'd improved by climbing every hill in the county behind her for the past month. Only two women were sticking with her on the climb. She and those women rode away from the rest of the field like the others were standing still. When Allie got to the switchbacks at the top of the climb, we went to the feed zone to wait for her.

She was still in first when they came zipping toward us. The difference in speed between Joe's class and this one was amazing. These women were *flying*.

"Want a bottle?" Joe yelled as Allie charged toward us.

"Next time," she yelled back without missing a pedal stroke.

"You're awesome!" we screamed at her receding backside.

The next lap, the same three women were together, but Allie looked strong and the other two looked tired. On the third lap, Allie had broken away from them and was leading the field by a good forty feet. We gave her a fresh water bottle filled with Gatorade, and she tossed an empty at us.

"Allie said she wants me to collect her prize money, if she wins any. Looks like she will." I grinned at Joe.

"Why? Why can't she do it?"

"She said she had to take off as soon as she's done."

"Weird," Joe said, "but okay. At least she's here."

On the last lap, I headed downhill to meet Allie at the finish line. Joe stayed back to offer her another bottle, and the crowd behind me, at the top of the hill, chanted "AllieCat! AllieCat! AllieCat!" These people knew her from lots of other mountain bike races. It gave me goose bumps, it was so cool.

I found a spot forty feet from the finish where I could see her come down the last descent, and then I could bolt to the finish line to meet her.

I saw the flash of her orange Kona bike through the trees and held my breath. She was as smooth as a wild animal coming through the woods. She'd cranked the speed, and nobody else was in sight.

Allie caught air, landed with her knees bent to absorb the shock, and rumbled down the patch of rocks and corduroy roots like a paint can in a shaker. She kept her knees cocked and her rear end low to hold her center of gravity over the back wheel, to keep it on the ground. Lots of air, lots of landings. There was one near miss when her back wheel slid sideways, but she steered into it, stayed on two wheels. She blasted into the last smooth downhill, hit the banked corner at well over twenty miles an hour, leaned into her turn, flew over the last jump, landed like a plane on a runway, then bent low over the handlebars and sped toward the finish line. No other riders were even out of the trees yet.

I ran toward the finish line at top speed. I'd been so mesmerized, watching her, I'd forgotten to be where she needed me to be. I was running, screaming, "You did it! You did it!"

She got her not-so-candid photo snapped by the newspaper, disentangled herself from the mob, and searched the crowd for me.

"Allie! Here! Allie!" I screamed. She heard me and relief flooded her face.

She pedaled over to me and ripped the number from the front of her bike. "I have to go *now*," she hissed. "Pretend I'm still here if anybody, *anybody* except Mike asks, until they give out the money, got it? Then make *sure* Mike gives it to *you*."

"Allie...you're incredible."

"Thanks, Sade. I felt good today. Please be there at four." And she was gone. Again.

TWENTY-FOUR

After Effects

July 4, continued

The other women rode in, exhausted and grimy with dust and sweat.

The one in second place crossed the finish line, put her feet down, and guzzled an entire bottle of Gatorade. The crowd roared for her, too, and when they quieted down, she looked around and said, "Where's that Allie-girl? She's not human."

She saw me and spun over. "That AllieCat kicks ass. You know where she went? She should think about going pro."

"She—she should be around here someplace." The lie felt small, but it stuck in my throat anyway. I wondered if Allie *could* go pro. If she could get sponsors and get paid to ride her bike.

The Expert women all came in closer together than the Beginners did, so the race was over within fifteen minutes after the time Allie finished. One woman rode in with a ripped jersey and dried blood on her shoulder and her knee—way worse than my crash.

The Men's Expert class was last. Joe went to the Luge descent to watch.

I stuck around at the bottom of the hill. The awards ceremony would start after most of the Expert men had finished.

I crammed Allie's number, and mine, into my jersey pocket and stashed all the rest of my stuff in the backpack beside my bike. Then I wandered around, killing time until awards. Volunteers were passing out free pizza slices for racers. I grabbed two slices and a cup of Pepsi and sat down on a picnic table bench. I stretched out my filthy legs, covered with sweat and dust mixed into a gritty paste. But here, dirt was a badge of accomplishment.

The pizza tasted *good*. I didn't realize how hungry I was. I could tell from the screams and cheers moving along the course that the Expert men were weaving along the top of the hill.

I soaked in the sun, feeling the warm pizza settle into my empty stomach, trying to absorb the fact that I'd actually gotten *third* in a race, glad to get to sit all by myself and bask.

A tall figure stepped into my sunlight, throwing the shadow of two long skinny legs over mine. I expected it to be another roadie, or somebody from my race—I didn't know anybody else here. I shaded my eyes and squinted upward, taking in ratty jeans, hands on his hips, and a T-shirt that read, *Polaris … at Breakneck Speed.*

This was no cyclist. When my eyes reached his Polaris cap, I felt as if I'd turned to stone right there in the glorious, victorious sunlight. My mouth was open to take another bite of the pepperoni pizza, but I was petrified—mouth hanging open, pizza dangling in my hand.

It was the weathered, leathery-looking man who'd ridden the four-wheeler ATV with the rednecks in the woods. The one who stared me down, whose eyes were like steel, the one Peapod wanted to rip limb from limb. I wished like crazy Peapod were here right now, because the eyes in front of me were *not* friendly.

"Where's Allison?" he said, his voice steady, like the controlled heat of molten steel in a foundry.

"Who?" I asked, squinting, my heart hammering while I tried to be cool and couldn't. Allie had said, *Pretend I'm still here if anybody, anybody except Mike asks.* Had she known this creep would show up? Could Allie know this guy?

"Don't play dumb with me. I know you two are thick as thieves."

In spite of the hot sun, my skin shrank with goose bumps. I could hear my heart hammering like it had going warp speed down the Mad Squirrel descent, like I needed to disappear *now*, melt into the picnic table. I supposed this tall leathery man could hear it hammering, too. "Who," I said, "are you?"

"Where is she?" The voice was carefully even, expecting to get what it demanded.

I lowered the pizza onto my paper plate. I wiped my mouth and hands on my napkin. "I don't…know…exactly."

"Don't give me that. I know you know." No change in his voice.

She told me to pretend. So I pretended. Pretended to be cool. "She's gotta be around here somewhere." I nearly choked on these words, couldn't stand to meet this guy's eyes. "She's probably waiting for the awards ceremony."

"I'd like to congratulate her. She raced so well."

I looked up at him.

His lips turned up in a thin smile, about as warm as his voice.

"Maybe…I don't know…maybe she's watching the men's downhill in the woods."

He didn't budge. He was waiting, like a steel trap, emotionless. I wished I were a better liar.

My heart and my palms felt like I was at the top of the downhill again. "Who are you?" I said again. "Why do you want Allie?"

The smile flattened into nothing, but his eyes didn't change whether his mouth was smiling or not. He looked at me as if he were boring holes through my head with those steel eyes. Then he turned and stalked away with a slight limp—long legs, skinny, with lean muscle visible through the faded jeans. His arms under his T-shirt sleeves were ripped and lean, like Peapod's rawhide bones, only leathery brown.

I picked up the pizza again, but I couldn't chew or swallow. Suddenly I wanted to collect our prizes and leave. I got up to go see Mike at the race director's tent. My legs were shaking, and the tent was empty.

"Whatcha need?" asked a familiar-looking guy in an unzipped jersey and bare feet, sitting on the grass in the shade of the tent, eating pizza.

"Just looking for Mike," I said. "Mike from A-1."

"He's inside." He nodded toward the bike shop. "They're in there figuring up the results. Be done pretty soon. I'm Mo-Jo. I met you at the bike shop."

I nodded. "I remember now. Thanks." So I was stuck here waiting for the awards ceremony if I wanted to get our prizes. Besides, I thought, it wasn't fair for that leathery man to wreck my fun. This was my first race, and I got third, so I should get to stand on the podium. I moved toward the center of the crowd, where *he* might not notice me, and where he wouldn't dare come bother me. I found the most crowded picnic table and stood beside it, pretending to watch for racers coming out of the woods. Finally, my stomach settled enough so I could swallow the rest of my pizza.

When the Men's Expert race was almost over, I went to stand by the finish line and watch Skarpohl and Big Brian swoop across the line. They got fifth and sixth.

Finally, finally, the officials tested the P.A. There were still riders out on the course, but they had all the results from the Expert race already. The guys still riding hadn't placed.

I couldn't find Joe, and I had a sick fear that the leather man had found him in the woods. Why did I tell the guy that Allie might be out in the woods? What if he got Joe all alone out there? Would he have any way of knowing who Joe was? He knew me, but he'd seen me in the woods. I turned and pushed through the crowd, paying no attention to the announcer who had started handing out awards. I was frantic to see Joe's face.

Somebody grabbed my jersey pocket from behind.

I whirled. "Joe! Ohmygosh," I almost cried. I hugged him instead.

"Sadie! What's wrong with you? Get going. They're calling your name!" I forgot to listen, and Beginner class was being announced first.

"Sadie Lester?" The P.A. crackled. "Is Sadie still here?"

I turned and broke from the crowd, trotting in my flip-flops toward the podium. I got to step up on the third step. The announcer draped a bronze medal around my neck, and he handed me a box with a new speedometer/odometer computer as my prize. Mike stepped over to the podium, too. "Way to go, Sadie." He shook my hand. "Good ride. AllieCat was right."

The guys who won second and first joined me. We all shook hands, and the newspaper photographer clicked our pictures. I smiled. I didn't have to pretend to be thrilled.

First place won a brand-new Time pedal and cleat system, and second won a pro helmet. Winners in the Beginner class didn't get money; it was incentive to move up to Sport if you were good enough. The reporter confirmed each of our names.

Then it hit me—the leathery man would know my name after he saw me in the newspaper, if he didn't already. The newspaper. That was it. If he knew Allie, and had seen her name in the paper in the article about Father Malcolm, my picture and Joe's were right there. No wonder he knew that I knew her.

Joe's race recognized ten places, but only paid money for the first five. He didn't care. He was so happy to have placed in the top twenty.

I bumped him with my shoulder. "Hey, come here." I led him to the side of the crowd so he could hear me. "Know who's here? The scary guy I saw on the four-wheeler in the woods—the guy riding with the rednecks. The one Peapod wanted to kill even more than the rednecks. He asked me where Allie—where *Allison*—is."

The P.A. system crackled. "Now for the Women's Expert class." This class paid through five places. The third-place woman stepped around me to go to the podium. She winked at me and muttered, "That race was like riding through hell."

"Great job," I said. It felt good to belong, like I had earned a place among the racers.

"Grand prize, first place, Women's Expert champion for the second year in a row, goes to Miss Allison Baker!" the announcer called. The crowd erupted in cheers, looking expectantly for Allie. "AllieCat! AllieCat!" a small group started chanting. The chant spread.

But of course there was no Allie.

I saw the leather man on the edge of the crowd, eyes riveted on me. I swallowed.

"Go," Joe shoved me. "What are you waiting for? Go get it."

"I thought I'd get it after the awards ceremony," I said to Joe over the din.

"Is Allison still here?" the announcer called.

The cheers faded.

"I'll take it," a voice boomed across the crowd. The leather, steel-eyed man strode toward the announcer. The announcer frowned at him, but the leather man reached out a hand. "I said I'd take it for her. I'm her father."

Her *father*? Allie's *father*? He was in prison. This couldn't be…

"NO!" I yelled. I ran toward the podium. "I'm supposed to collect her prize. She asked me to. You can't give it to him!" I looked up at the leathery man. "Who are you really?"

He chuckled. It was as metallic sounding as his voice. "Don't be a wiseass. I'm Allison's father. I'm collecting her prize for her."

Everything jumbled around in my head. Her father. In prison. Allie taking off without an explanation... Her father? Out of prison? *Breaking the law...What else?* Allie had said.

"NO!" I said again. I turned back to the announcer, yanked Allie's number from my jersey pocket, and pleaded, "She gave me this. She told me to collect her prize for her. You *have* to believe me." The announcer looked from me to the man, confused, holding the envelope, not relinquishing it to either of us.

"I'll just take it for her." The steel and leather man snaked out a lanky arm. The announcer pulled the envelope back out of his reach. The leather man's eyes grew harder, even more like steel, if that were possible. Without taking those eyes off the official, he fished a wallet out of his skinny jeans and held out a driver's license. "Cecil Baker," he said. "Allison Baker's my daughter."

"You *can't* give it to him." I shoved Allie's number at the announcer, in front of the driver's license. "Allie wants *me* to pick it up."

Just then, Mike of A-1 Bike stepped up beside the announcer. "Sorry, sir. We'll just keep the prize money. I'll deliver it directly to the champion myself."

"What?" I deflated. "Mike, Allie asked me—"

"Trust me," Mike said. "Sorry sir. Sorry, Sadie, I can't give this out to anyone other than Allie herself."

The man's steel eyes bore holes into Mike's face. He turned and strode through the crowd, which parted like a sweaty sea. He went straight toward the parking lot and didn't look back. The crowd was silent.

"All right then," said the announcer. "Let's hear it for the women ... Next and last, we have the Men's Expert class."

The man disappeared, and I turned back to Mike. "That's not really her dad, is it?"

"Yup. Afraid so."

"I thought he was ... in prison."

"He was."

"He's *out*?"

Mike looked at me and nodded meaningfully, as if he wanted me to read his face without asking any more questions.

"Holy shit." My mind couldn't keep up with all the ideas spinning around. Her dad. Her disappearance. I couldn't put it all together. "Mike. You still have to give me the prize money. I promised Allie. She said you'd give it to me."

"Nope. No way. Not since he showed up. That dude is dangerous. I'll take the money to her."

"So you *do* know where to find her! I thought so. Tell me."

He bit both lips, as if locking them, and shook his head.

"Come on, Mike. She's at your bike shop, isn't she?"

"Listen Sadie. I appreciate your loyalty and your dedication. Allie will, too. But believe me, it's better if you don't know where she is. Safer that way."

"Safer? But—she'll be waiting for me."

"You want that dude following you?"

"No, but—"

"If he knows you're taking money to her, you think he won't follow you?" He shook his head again. "No way. Where were you going to meet her?"

"Back door of A-1."

"See? Nothing suspicious about me being at my own shop on a holiday. You? Yes."

"Four o'clock," I said, defeated.

"I got it covered, Sadie."

"Okay. Shoot," I said. "She was going to tell me the whole story when I came to meet her. Tell her ... tell her I would have brought it."

"You got it. And I'll tell her I wouldn't let you keep your promise."

I drifted back to Joe like I was in a fog. Joe grabbed my arm. "Allie's *father?* That dude is *scary.*"

"You're not kidding. Joe, come here." I motioned him over to the side of the crowd so we could talk. "That's not even half of it. He's been in prison."

"What? Prison?"

"Stillwater Prison."

"I didn't mean *what prison*. You knew he was in prison, and you never told me?" he said.

"It didn't occur to me."

"All this time we've been looking for her. Don't you think it might matter if her dad was in prison?"

"Well, it doesn't exactly change anything, does it? I didn't think it had anything to do with her disappearing. He's locked away and all—and we don't know why he's there—was there—she wouldn't tell me that—just that he's in Stillwater."

"But now it matters. 'Cause he's obviously *out.* You think there's a connection? Her leaving and her dad being out?"

"Why? Joe, how would that matter? It was the priest that made her take off, not her dad."

"This just gets deeper and more screwed up all the time."

We stared at each other, letting everything soak in, wracking our brains.

"You think," I asked, "that it was him watching us this morning? When Peapod growled?"

Joe shrugged. "No reason to think it was him, really. I think we're creeping ourselves out."

"We were right about Mike anyway," I said. "He knows where Allie is. He's taking her money to her. I think she's been staying at the bike shop."

✖✖

When everything was over, we loaded our backpacks. We turned our bikes out of the parking lot, toward the river and the bike path shortcut to LeHillier.

Where the bike trail forked at Highway 66, a green diesel pickup sat at the stop sign, blocking the trail that crossed the highway. Smoke wafted in the shimmery heat from the driver's window. A cigarette mirage of wavy air.

We both did track stands at the stop sign, waiting for the traffic on the highway so the pickup could go. When it was the pickup's turn, he did not move.

"Holy crap," Joe said under his breath. "It's him!"

The leathery man looked at us, took a drag on his cigarette, and blew smoke straight at us. "You lied to me," he said.

I swallowed.

"You can tell me now where my daughter is."

"I didn't lie. I don't know where Allie is." I swallowed hard. Again. "Today's the first time I've seen Allie since ... since ... "

"Since what?"

"Since Fath—" I cut myself off. "For several days," I finished. "Since the last time we rode together."

He stared. "Since what? What were you going to say? And if you don't know where she is, how were you going to give her the money? You were just going to steal it, weren't you?"

"No! I was going to meet her—"

"Let's go, Sadie." Joe said. Since the truck blocked the trail crossing entirely, he veered his bike to go behind and around the pickup, but the man jammed the truck into reverse. "Holy crap." Joe slammed on his brakes.

"Answer my question, young lady." The man gunned his engine. The memory of the rednecks chasing Allie and me washed over me.

"There's nothing to say," I said. "'Cause I'm not meeting her now. I don't have her money, and I don't know where she is. Leave me alone. Come on, Joe. Let's go this way." I turned my bike around, back toward Mount Kato. Joe followed.

The leathery man opened the driver's door and in one fluid motion, was halfway across the pavement toward us.

"Shit!" Joe said. "Come on!"

We took off as fast as our tired legs would accelerate. Allie's dad lunged for my bike, but he missed. By inches. For a man with a limp, he moved with catlike smoothness. And speed. Allie's father, indeed. We rode, adrenaline pumping our legs as fast as in any race sprint.

He chased us for about twenty feet. I didn't look back, but I could hear his boots on the trail, running and then stopping. I could feel his eyes boring into my back until we crested the hill out of sight, back to the ski hill parking lot. We coasted in among the remaining crowd.

"Joe. You said *shit*!"

"Yeah. I know." Joe braked and put a shaky foot down. "I think that was shit-worthy."

It was one of those moments so full of tension that we had to bust wide open, crying or laughing. We burst out laughing. Our legs shook, and we laughed so hard we almost fell over. "Ya know, it's not funny at all," I said. "I'm scared to death." And we laughed all the harder.

"We better get going," Joe said. "Especially if we have to go the long way home, through town."

And so we rode the bike trail into Mankato and back around main roads to LeHillier. We looked over our shoulders all the way. No sign of the green pickup.

We finally turned into Scout's driveway. I'd never been so happy to smell burgers and hear my little cousins' voices. We wheeled our bikes into the garage.

"I feel like a limp noodle," Joe said. "I got nothin' left."

"I'm still shaking." I hung my bike on the hooks Scout had installed. "What do we do now?"

When I turned, Joe was standing only inches from me. "How 'bout this?" He held out his arms and pulled me into a hug. We stood there, trying to let the tension leak away.

Finally, I looked up into Joe's face. He smiled down into mine, ran his index knuckle along my jaw. "For starters," he whispered, "I'm proud of you today. And I'm so glad you're okay. Cecil Baker is one scary dude."

I nodded, feeling his chin against my head. His arms felt good.

"Thanks for listening to me this morning. Seems like a long time ago."

"You're welcome. I'm glad you talked to me. And Joe? You did it. You went down the big hill. Like nothing."

And then, he took my chin in his hand and lifted my face toward his.

"John would be proud," I whispered.

"I hope so." He looked into my eyes. Finally, finally he was going to kiss me, and I was not about to screw it up. I lifted my chin and closed my eyes.

"Sadie! Joe! Where are you?" Uncle Scout bellowed from right outside the garage door. "I thought I saw you ride up."

We pulled apart as quickly as we'd gotten away from Cecil Baker. And started to laugh again. We couldn't help it. "Scout!" Joe called through his laughter. "In the garage."

"And what are you doin' in here?" Scout said. "Come get a burger. Your grandma's here, too, waiting to see you, Sadie. How did the race go? And what's so funny?"

So we told him. We told him everything we knew.

Except, of course, about why we were laughing.

TWENTY-FIVE

Rockin' in the Quarry

The Fourth of July

By the time we finished our story, Scout had chewed clear through his cigar. "F—Blast it all." Since jail, Scout had embraced an anti-swearing campaign in addition to his anti-drinking campaign. It was tough on him. "What do you think this has to do with Allie disappearing? Think she's hiding from her own dad?"

"No idea. But I'd hide from that dude, if I was her," Joe said.

"Makes sense," I said. "All she ever said is that her dad was in prison. I got the feeling that she doesn't exactly feel warm and fuzzy about the guy. Like something bad enough happened that she won't talk about it. Or him."

Scout bit another piece off his cigar and spit it out the garage door. "You two okay?"

We nodded. "A little shaky is all," I said.

"And hungry," Joe added.

"What am I thinking! I put burgers on the grill for you when I saw you coming up the hill," Scout said. "Might be burnt offerings by now. You go eat. I'm going to call the cops."

"But—" I started.

"Nope. No arguments. I'm calling. Tell 'em what we know. Go."

So we did.

I ate two cheeseburgers from the grill. I'd never eaten two whole burgers before, but I was starving in spite of the pizza I'd had. Scout's burgers, in the bar or at home, were legendary. Thomas made the best potato salad in the country, and Grandma had brought apple and peach pie to our picnic. It was quite the spread.

Grandma sat next to me at the picnic table and patted my grimy leg.

"Watch out, Grandma, I'm pretty stinky."

"I don't care about that. Tell me about the race."

"Sadie was amazing," Joe chimed in.

Susan poured rock salt into the hand-crank ice cream maker. Timmy and Stevie took turns cranking for her. "Was Allie there?" she asked.

"Yeah. She got first by about a mile." We told the race stories. We stopped at the finish line.

Susan looked as if she might cry. "This ice cream just won't set up. It'll just be cream soup!" she said. "Stevie, you have to crank faster. Or let me crank."

"You can do it," Stevie said. He and Timmy took off running. Smart boys, I thought.

"Susan, you worry too much," Grandma said. "My stars, I survived Scout *and* Thomas *and* this one's mama." She patted my dirty leg again. "Runny ice cream is small potatoes. Not worth fretting."

Susan brushed hair out of her face with the back of her hand but didn't look up. Josie chose that moment to ask, "Are we shooting the cannon *boom* today?"

I thought that was a hilarious question, but Joe and I were the only ones who laughed. Susan looked up and glared at us. So did Janie.

"Oops," muttered Joe.

I swallowed to keep from laughing again. "Yeah," I said to Josie. "There'll be lots of booms. But Scout said they only shoot oatmeal cannon balls in the quarry. It's safe."

Susan cranked the ice cream bucket even harder.

"Well." I got up. "Time to go take a shower." I gave Grandma a peck on the cheek.

Joe followed me. He whispered, "Is Aunt Susan certifiably nuts? Who cares about mushy ice cream? I never knew she was so moody before this summer."

We met Scout in the kitchen. "Cecil Baker is out on parole," he said. "That's worse than probation. He's only been out of prison about eight days. Cops said they're keeping an eye on him. Will you do me a favor? Keep me posted where you are all the time. Joe, you have your cell phone?"

"Yup."

"Scout?" I said. "Maybe you shouldn't tell Aunt Susan about Allie's dad. She's stressed out enough already."

He nodded. "Probably right. Now go clean up. We gotta leave for Rockin' in the Quarry pretty quick. You two can meet us out there."

❊❊

Rockin' in the Quarry was a sight to behold. Thousands—literally thousands and thousands—of people packed into the flat bottom of the quarry on blankets and lawn chairs, or perched on coolers.

Blue Velveeta, a popular local band, belted out "Party in My Mind." A couple dozen people were dancing by the stage when Joe and I wandered in.

The quarry was about half a mile wide and looked like it was a mile long. One side, the stone cutters had taken away slabs of Kasota stone—a special local limestone—for things like pillars, stone steps, the "Welcome to Mankato" monolith, and the huge "Minnesota State University" markers. The outcroppings left behind made a natural backdrop for a stone stage. On the far back side, behind the mob, there were mountains of crushed gravel, five stories high, where little kids were scrambling up and sliding down. Between the performance stage and the gravel mountains, the floor of this whole place was flat.

We walked up and down among picnic blankets, coolers, lawn chairs, and umbrellas looking for Susan and Janie in the mob. Uncle Scout and Uncle Thomas spied us and waved from their post by the cannon, between the crowd and the gravel mountains. Thomas mopped his sweaty forehead with a white monogrammed hanky.

I jabbed Joe in the ribs. "Look at Thomas's hanky. Guess that means it's a *dress* occasion, calling for a dress hanky."

Joe snorted. "Those guys are something, aren't they?" We waved back.

Blue Velveeta launched into "Lawyers, Guns and Money," and the place went wild.

Joe smiled. "This is great."

"Imagine how much more fun it would be if we weren't worried sick about Allie. You think she ever gets lost in a crowd to hide?"

Joe squeezed my hand. "Doesn't seem like something she'd do, but who knows? Maybe we'll see her."

Scout waved to us again and pointed into the crowd. Joe dropped my hand. I followed Scout's finger and spied Aunt Susan and Aunt Janie on a blanket, along with all seven little kids and Grandma in her lawn chair. Timmy waved frantically at us.

We made our way over to them just in time to join the screaming standing ovation for Blue Velveeta. Joe and I squeezed in on the blanket beside Stevie and Timmy. The band played "He Be Gee Bees" as an encore, and then the Mankato Symphony started setting up.

✖ ✖

Our hand-holding didn't get past Timmy. As soon as we sat down, he fairly screamed in a whisper, "You were *holding Joe's hand!*" I looked at Timmy's face, trying to decide whether he approved, or was appalled and grossed out.

"So?" I said.

"So, is he your *boyfriend*?"

"Ah ... " I glanced at Joe. "Not really—"

"Would it be okay with you?" Joe asked. He leaned across my lap toward Timmy.

"Would what be okay?" Timmy said.

"Would it be okay if your sister was my girlfriend?" He put his hand on my knee and grinned at Timmy.

My chest thumped. Timmy's eyes got huge. He straightened up and his chest puffed up. "Really?" he asked.

My heart was hammering in my ears now.

"She's the coolest girl I know," Joe said. "And the prettiest."

My face got about a hundred degrees hotter.

Timmy grinned. "Yeah. But she can be a pain in the butt, too," he said.

"Big sisters are supposed to be a pain in the butt," said Joe. "That's their job. Your sister's cool, though. You don't know what a real pain in the butt is like."

"Okay." Timmy leaned against my arm. "It's okay if you're her boyfriend. You're not really cousins, are you?"

"Ha." Joe said. "Nope. Not at all. Just happen to have married relatives."

Timmy scrunched up his eyebrows, figuring this out. "Oh. Okay."

I wasn't sure if Joe had been teasing Timmy or if he was serious. Joe shrugged and smiled into my eyes. "So. I s'pose I should ask you. You wanna be my girlfriend?" He picked up my hand and held it between both of his.

I let all the air out of my torso. It felt like I'd been holding my breath for a long, long time. "I think so," I said.

He smiled. "Okay then." He ran his thumb over the back of my hand, and this time, it didn't just feel good, it was electric. It was like heat and cold all at once, and it ran up my arm and to all sorts of surprising places, *all over my body*, and for cryin' out loud, he was only touching my *hand*.

"Is it a secret?" Timmy whispered to us.

"Kind of," Joe said. "We're not telling Aunt Susan yet."

"Okay," Timmy said, and he scootched over so he was sitting between our hands and Aunt Susan. "I'll cover you up!"

We laughed. "Thanks, Buddy," Joe said.

So there I sat, speechless, holding Joe's hand, in cahoots with my little brother as the symphony began their first piece: "Rhapsody in Blue" by Gershwin, a jazzy piece from Walt Disney's *Fantasia*.

Allie was a nagging worry at the back of my head, but there was nothing I could do for her at this moment. I felt good letting myself relax. When Joe let go of my hand, I leaned back on my elbows and rested my legs. I was aware of Joe filling the space beside me. That felt good, too.

After "Stars and Stripes Forever" and "Medley from *The Music Man*," Joe leaned toward me. "Want to go walk around? Get a hot dog or something? I'm hungry again."

"Is that something new?" I gave his shoulder a friendly push.

"I want a hot dog!" Timmy said to Joe.

"Me too," Stevie said.

"Me, too," Megan chimed in.

"Holy crap, what did I start?" Joe muttered.

"Nope." Janie held out a Tupperware bowl of cookies. "We already ate. You guys stay with us. Let Joe and Sadie go if they want." Janie actually winked at me. I wondered what got into her to be nice to me, but I wasn't going to ask.

I caught Susan's eye and pointed toward the food stands, and she nodded back.

"We'll be back," I told Timmy. He didn't protest. His mouth was jammed full of chocolate chip cookie.

Joe and I walked around the perimeter of the crowd. Stands selling cotton candy, footlongs, kettle corn, elephant ears, tacos, homemade taffy. Anything we wanted, as long as it had at least thirty grams of fat per serving. We each bought a Polish sausage and a Coke. We sat and ate at some benches, out of sight of the family and all the little kids who would want what we had if they saw us.

A guy with brown spikey hair who looked vaguely familiar came hurrying over, dragging his girlfriend by the hand. The girlfriend wore lots of eye make-up, a white halter top with her tummy sticking out over her shorts, skinny legs below with no muscle tone, and a look of absolute boredom on her face.

"Sadie. Nice job today," the guy said.

I swallowed a big bite of sausage and bun. "Thanks."

"I'm Rob. I was in your race. You passed me on the switchback. Remember?"

"Oh, I wouldn't have recognized you," I said. "But thanks."

"Hey, what was the deal with that Allie girl's dad?" Rob asked. The girlfriend rolled her eyes.

"No idea. Really." I stood up. "Hey, Joe, come on. The orchestra's starting Mozart. Last song before the *1812 Overture*. We gotta go so we don't miss the cannon. Excuse us. See you, Rob."

"Nice brush-off," Joe said.

"Allie's dad is the *last* thing I want to talk about."

We skirted around the outside edge of the crowd on our way back to the family. Near the gravel mountains, behind all the lawn chairs and blankets, a hayrack was hooked to a pickup. A canopy covered the rack, with about a dozen people and several coolers among the hay bales. All the guys leaning on the rack were shirtless. They nodded and grinned at us. One of the guys whistled, and Joe put his arm around my shoulder as we passed.

We turned the corner and grinned at each other. "Everybody thinks you're hot. See?" Joe said into my ear. "This is fun." We weren't watching where we were walking and almost ran smack into two guys without shirts.

"Watch it," the one wearing a Schlitz cap said.

"Sorry," Joe said.

"Well, well. It's the little nosey bitch who won't get off the road," the other one said. He was wearing a Vikings hat. It was the reptilian ponytail guy.

The rednecks.

I stopped dead, frozen. The last people I expected at a concert. And now, now I knew what I hadn't thought about since the race—hadn't fully realized until this moment, when everything about these guys came rushing back. These two asshole rednecks had been riding ATVs with Cecil Baker. They were *friends* with Allie's dad.

"Watch where you're walkin'. And you"—the Schlitz cap redneck poked a finger at me—"you and Miss High-and-Mighty Strong Arm Miss Allison Baker—keep your noses out of where they don't belong."

"If you know what's good for you," the reptilian guy threw in. The driver elbowed him hard in the ribs, and he collapsed inward at the blow. "Jeez, ya don't have to get violent. I'm just sayin'—"

I felt myself shrinking back, instinctively clinging tighter to Joe's hand.

The driver went on, "Mr. Cecil Baker has a message for his daughter, if you would deliver it, please. He'd like his daughter to come home." Here his tone changed to sickly sweet. "He misses his baby." His sick smile evaporated. "Now you tell her that. Ya hear?"

"And," the reptilian guy straightened up again to say, "you tell her Cecil Baker is *not* going back to the slammer. Period. No matter what anybody says to frame him—"

"Will you *shut up*!" The driver elbowed him again.

"Back off." The voice was so authoritative, it made me jump. "Leave her alone." I looked up. Joe. Joe, my new boyfriend, released my hand, pulled himself to his full height, and was chest-to chest with the ponytail guy. "*You* leave my girlfriend alone, or you'll really, really wish you had."

My mouth fell open. Joe, who was a self-proclaimed wuss, Joe, who apologized for not being fearless, Joe, who had just asked my little brother if I could be his girlfriend, Joe, my new boyfriend, stuck his finger in the driver's face. "You touch her again, or threaten her on her bike, you'll be dead. You understand? Now *back off*!"

If the rednecks' eyes had flashed fear when confronted with Scout and Thomas, now their eyes flashed surprise and shock. The element of ambush took them off guard so completely that they only stammered as Joe grabbed my hand and we walked right past the two jerks.

"Back off. You'll really wish you had," the rednecks called after us, trying to mock Joe, but the words bounced off our backs as we strode away.

We headed into the crowd until we'd gotten a safe distance away.

"Joe." I yanked on his hand. "I can't believe you. I mean, I can hardly believe you said that to those assholes. How—why—how could you do that? Talk about guts."

"I don't know," Joe said. "I'm shaking now."

"You were awesome." I squeezed his hand. "And now we know they're Allie's dad's friends."

"And now we know for sure that Allie's not at her house, wherever that is."

"What do you think they were talking about? Frame Cecil Baker? He's already been in and out of prison," I said. "Those guys are so nuts, they don't even make any sense."

Joe said, "Do you think she recognized them? Back when they ran you guys off the road?"

"No. I'm sure she didn't. She would have said something, don't you think? I mean, the way she came storming into the Last Chance."

Joe started to chuckle. "That was my introduction to Allie." He smiled down at me. "And to you, for that matter, besides at the truck stop."

At that moment, the cellos started the sad, somber notes of the *1812 Overture*. The big-boy uncles would shoot their cannon soon.

"We better hurry," I said.

"Or," Joe said, "we could stand right here and listen and watch."

We looked over at the aunts and little kids. They were absorbed in the music and watching the cannons. They weren't looking our direction.

The uncles were very busy with their toys.

"Okay," I said. "We can see everything from here."

Uncle Thomas was checking something on the cannon. Then the Union soldier guys, in their blue coats, stood at attention, trying not to wiggle like little boys.

The music sounded like a hymn, and then it grew into this horrible, wonderful, awful collision of notes that really sounded like a battle. This song was written by Tchaikovsky, the same guy who wrote *The Nutcracker*. I knew *The Nutcracker* because I was in ballet for six years, until I got the guts to tell my mom I'd rather ride my bike after school than take dance lessons.

I loved this music, but I didn't very often admit that to anybody. I slid my hand up under Joe's arm and stood on tiptoes to say in his ear, "I love this song."

Joe squeezed my hand against his ribs. "I'll pay attention then."

At the height of the music that painted a battle scene, Scout brought a match (no cigar this time) to the powder hole, and though I didn't want to move my hand away from Joe, I did. I watched Timmy and the other little cousins sit up straight. We covered our ears, as did lots of people around us, and we watched the flare and the shudder, and flame shooting from the cannon barrel. The *boom* crashed inside my eardrums and in my sternum, even through the palms of my hands, and even with an oatmeal cannonball.

In spite of my eardrums, I could hear the music roaring bloodshed and gunfire, drums, strings, and deep brass, as the cannons went off again and again. They filled the air with explosion, smoke, and dust. I looked at Joe, his hands over his ears, and I yelled, "Joe, you know what? What you did tonight? Standing up to those guys? You're anything but a wuss."

He grinned and took his hands off his ears. He practically had to yell for me to hear. "Nobody gets to treat you like that and get away with it."

And with the cannons crashing around us, and in the middle of all the dust and music and smoke, and in sight of Susan and Janie and Timmy and God and everyone, Joe took my chin in his hand and lifted my face to his. And he kissed me. And we didn't get interrupted.

My knees were already weak from terror, exhaustion, the race, adrenaline coming and going all day, and now this last run-in with the rednecks. When Joe brought his lips to mine, I was sure they would give out entirely. If he hadn't had his arms wrapped around me, I thought I might have landed on the dusty quarry floor. I didn't know lips could feel strong. But they did. Soft and strong all at once. But then his tongue flicked against mine and he pulled me tighter, and I forgot all about my knees.

The cannons roared and thundered, the dust rose, the music swelled around us, and his mouth melded to mine. And I felt it everywhere.

TWENTY-SIX

Ice Cream

The Fourth of July, continued

Nobody saw us kiss. Everybody was too busy watching the cannons and listening and covering their ears to pay any attention to us. Timmy included.

Timmy and Stevie begged to ride home with us from the concert. I would have liked fifteen minutes alone with Joe, but Joe looked at me, shrugged, and said, "Okay. Come on." The little guys jumped up and down, so I felt guilty for not wanting them to come.

Driving home, I sat in the passenger seat like before, but now it felt different. If I was Joe's girlfriend, should I sit next to him? I looked at the spot on the seat right next to him, where girlfriends usually sit in front seats, and the magnetic pull to be close to him was electric. I slid a little closer. As much as my seat belt would allow.

I'd had a boyfriend last year, Kevin, but he'd just asked me, "You want to go out with me?" and it meant we talked on the phone, sat together at basketball games, and danced at school dances. We watched movies in his basement three times, and he only gave me a quick peck on the lips each of those evenings. Mom wouldn't let us be alone together if she could help it. "Too young," she'd said. We were both fourteen when we started dating, fifteen when we broke up.

This was different.

And I wondered if I was a selfish, horrible person to be feeling all this when Allie was hiding somewhere. I had no idea where, and I wasn't even sure why, except now I thought it must have something to do with scary leather-dude dad. But here I was, basking in the glow of Joe's attention, wanting nothing more than for him to touch me again, the whole world looking more vibrant because Joe liked me, and because I'd raced and done okay, and all the while, Allie was in some subterranean hideout under my feet. What was wrong with me?

But, I tried to tell myself, Allie was the strong one, strong enough to hold up, even holed up.

Going up the last hill to Scout's, Stevie leaned forward and squealed, "Look! Fireworks!"

Bottle rockets flared above the trees, a bouquet of illegal color from the junk woods. Colored sparks showered down toward the road and Joe slowed to avoid them. Somebody must have cleaned out his car right there: bottles and paper and cans and Dairy Queen containers heaped by the shoulder of the road. Joe and I shook our heads at each other.

When we pulled into the driveway and got out of the car, firecrackers crackled in the woods like popcorn popping.

"Can we do firecrackers?" Timmy asked.

"Nope," I said. "Too dangerous with so many kids around. We're going to go watch the big fireworks later, though."

Timmy ran after Stevie into the house. They came running back out, whooping before we'd even gotten to the steps. "Sparklers! Look, Sadie!"

Scout produced eight boxes of sparklers, and the boys and Megan swirled arcs and circles of color in the yard and wrote their names against the sky.

I cornered Scout and told him about the rednecks at Rockin' in the Quarry. And about how Joe stood up to them, without telling exactly what Joe had said.

"Good man, that Joe," Scout put a new unlit cigar in this mouth. He winked at me. I wondered if he knew, or guessed. My uncle was no dummy.

Aunt Susan's homemade ice cream had finally frozen, so Joe and I dished up ice cream for the kids, dropping a Hershey's Kiss upside down in each cone. Firework explosions from the trailer court made a constant backdrop of noise and flashes through the kitchen window. Joe tilted his head toward the sound. "Reminds me of the concert. Like we're in a battle zone."

"Take the ice cream outside to eat it," Janie hollered from the living room.

"Yes!" Stevie and Timmy bolted out, balancing ice cream.

"I'm so scared for Allie," I said. "I can't stop thinking about her."

"Me neither."

Outside, Megan screamed. A blood-curdling, scared-within-an-inch-of-her-of-her-life scream, and Joe and I looked at each other.

"Cecil!" I dropped the ice cream scoop and we ran.

Around the corner toward the garage, Megan stood, ice cream cone upside down, as a little garter snake swirled like a green ribbon across the sidewalk.

"Oh!" I felt myself deflate with relief, felt the tension drop a few notches, and I could hear Joe let out his breath behind me. He stepped around me, nabbed the little snake behind the head, and carried him, curling and writhing, to the edge of the trees.

Megan's lip pooched out. Her ice cream had splatted onto the sidewalk. "It stuck out its tongue at me!" she screeched.

"Yeah," I said. "That's what snakes do. But ya know what? They're a lot scareder of you than you are of them. That's why they stick out their tongues. 'Cause they're so scared. If you don't touch them, little snakes like that won't touch you."

Joe came back. "Little garter snake squiggled away in the grass as fast as he could go," he said to Megan. "He was terrified. He's never heard so much racket."

"Then maybe he won't come back." Megan looked at Joe, then at me, skeptically but wanting to believe us. "He was scareder?" she asked.

"He sure was," Joe said.

Finally relaxed enough to realize her ice cream loss, Megan screwed up her face to let out a wail, but I interrupted the dramatics. "Want new a new cone? We'll get you a brand-new one."

She nodded.

"Peapod!" Joe yelled. "Ice cream for you."

Peapod came galumphing, happy and wagging, and found the ice cream with one sniff. He plunked down on the sidewalk, straddling it with his forelegs, and lapped it up with his giant tongue. I patted him on the butt and we went back inside.

When the last little kid ran outside with an ice cream cone, Joe said, "I guess my imagination is working overtime. I thought for sure—"

"Me, too."

He kissed me on the temple. Susan walked into the kitchen and missed it by about half a second.

Everybody finished ice cream and trooped inside to wash sticky fingers and put on long sleeves against the inevitable mosquito onslaught at the big fireworks display, held up on the Minnesota State University campus.

The phone rang. Scout looked at Joe and me, and answered it in the kitchen. He kept looking at us. "Yes...I see...of course...thank you." He stood quietly by the phone for a moment, then motioned us outside. "That was a nurse at the hospital. It seems that Father Malcolm is taking a turn. His vitals look worse, but he seems to be waking up."

"Why did they call here?" Joe asked.

"I asked the nurses to call if there was any change. And the doctors said it was okay to put us on the call list."

"Great," I said. "Thanks."

"You have any idea where Allie is?"

"Only an idea," I said.

"And that is...?"

"I think at A-1 Bike Shop. Mike knew where to find her, and that's where she wanted me to meet her, so it's the only place I can guess. And now we know for sure that she's not at home."

"My guess," Scout said, "is that you're right. I think maybe you should go together, pick her up, and trek up to the hospital. I don't think she should be alone out on her bike tonight. And I think it would be good for her to see you, and good for Father Malcolm to see her."

We stared at him.

"And I'd catch holy hell if I ditched the family right now to go with you, or else I would. Deal?"

Joe and I looked at each other. "Okay," we said in unison, but without much confidence.

"Got your cell phone, Joe?"

Joe nodded.

"Call me when you've got Allie. Call me when you get to the hospital. Call me when you leave, okay? No funny business. Keep me posted. If there's an emergency, I'll come on the double. We'll take two vehicles and Thomas can handle the women and kids. Fireworks are at ten. Just bring Allie along when you come back. Do her good to hang out with all of us crazies for the show. She'll think her own situation isn't quite so bad. Maybe."

"You didn't meet Cecil," I reminded him.

I called A-1 Bike. I knew Allie wouldn't answer the phone, but if she was in there, she might hear a message on the answering machine. "Allie. Joe and I are coming to pick you up. Back door of A-1. Five minutes from now. We got a phone call from the hospital about Father Malcolm. We'll knock at the back door."

So we set off.

We parked behind A-1, where Allie had told me to come at four o'clock. It was dark, dark, in the alley, but there were quite a few cars, probably for the bar two doors down. We sat in the car for a couple minutes. Nothing looked too suspicious, so we got out, locked Joe's car, and walked up the rickety wooden steps to A-1's back door.

We went into the entryway, like she'd told me to do. A dim light burned above us, cigarette butts littered the edges of the floor, and a stairway led up into the darkness. We knocked at the steel door in front of us.

Ferocious barking erupted inside, behind the door. We jumped back, from instinct. The dog, whoever it was, sounded like he could tear us limb from limb, and the barking was interspersed with snarling and dog nails against the door. We knocked again, and the snarling increased.

"Allie?" I called, softly but trying to be heard over the dog. We could tell when somebody came up and touched, or was holding, the dog. The scratching stopped and the occasional barks were muffled. "Allie!" I called louder. "It's Sadie. And Joe. Allie?"

The door cracked open. "Sadie? Get in here."

The dog's mouth was all I could see, and it reminded me of a skill saw. The shop was dark except for the neon bike signs on the back wall and in the front window. I didn't like the idea of stepping into the dark toward that mouth, but Allie hissed, "I've got Siren. Get in here." She shoved the door open another couple inches.

Joe and I squeezed through the door, and Allie motioned to shut it. Joe pushed it closed.

"Shh," Allie said to the dog. "Siren, be quiet." The dog sat down immediately, docile, and let his tongue hang out. He looked up at Allie with nothing but adoration.

"Siren?" I said, my eyes adjusting to the dark.

He wagged at me.

"He didn't know it was you," Allie said. "Joe, bolt the door, will you?"

Joe bolted it.

"We know that dog," I said.

"He followed you away from the hospital," Joe said.

"And he was hanging around when the police came after we found Father Malcolm," I said. "So, this is Siren."

Allie nodded and rubbed Siren's head. "He won't hurt a flea. Except if that flea hurts me." She grinned.

"Jeez, he looks like he'd rip our heads off," Joe said.

"He's probably capable," Allie said. "He hates my dad. Probably thought it was him knocking. Siren, meet Sadie. And Joe."

I forced myself to reach out my hand, palm down, and Siren licked it. I touched his head and he wagged. Joe gave him a pat, too.

Allie let go of his collar. He came over and sniffed my knees and Joe's shoes, and then he went back and leaned against Allie's leg.

"Has your dad been here?" I said. "And what are *you* doing here? Have you been here all the time?"

"My dad? No. Me, yeah. Seemed like a safe place. And Mike let me stay."

"Why didn't you tell us? Why did you hide from us?" I asked.

"Because you met my dad today. Mike told me," she said. "And you could tell him you didn't know where I was. Right?"

We nodded.

"And I figured you're a lousy liar. If you'd known where I was, my dad would have gotten it out of you somehow. Trust me on this one. I figured he'd find you eventually, since his asshole friends that chased us know we're friends, and the only way you'd be safe is if you really didn't know where I was. I didn't know what else to do. And I had to stick around town to win the race, so I'd have enough money to run away."

"You *did* know those rednecks."

"I don't *know* them, but I recognized them."

"Allie, did you know your dad was there? At the race?"

"Nope. Not 'til Mike told me. I didn't see him. But I figured he would show up, knowing I wouldn't miss it."

"So tell us. Why in the heck did you take off after you saw Father Malcolm?" I had so many questions I didn't know where to start.

"Wait," Joe said. "Father Malcolm! Allie, he might be waking up ... or dying ... while we stand here."

"What? What are you talking about?"

"That's why we're here. The hospital called Scout. The nurse said he was 'taking a turn.' Getting worse but sort of waking up. Scout said we should come get you and go see him."

"Holy smoke. Okay, let's go. But I need to leave town tonight. Before my dad figures out where I am. He probably already knows. I bet he followed you. I'm sure he's been watching you, once he figured out who you are."

Joe looked at me. We both thought about the woods this morning when Peapod growled, but we didn't say it out loud.

"Allie, I'm so confused—"

"Me, too," Joe said, "but I think we should get going to the hospital. We can talk in the car. Allie, how are you leaving? I mean, to run away? You only have a bike. Are you taking Siren?"

"Siren can keep up with me for ten miles, if I don't go too fast. I figured we'd get to St. Peter tonight, sleep somewhere, Le Sueur the next night, then Henderson... till we figured something out."

"You don't make any sense, Allie. Where are you *going*?"

"I don't know. Anywhere away from here. Away from my dad. If he finds me, for starters, he'll kill Siren. And I will *not* go to another foster home. I'd rather die. And I won't go anywhere without Siren."

"Come stay with us. Uncle Scout said you should come home with us," I said.

"No way. All those little kids? You don't want my dad near Scout's with all those little kids."

"He wouldn't hurt—" Joe started.

Allie whirled on him. "And what do you know about that? You do *not* know my father!" Her chest heaved. "He..."

Joe and I stared at her, waiting for her to finish.

"Come on," Allie said. "We've gotta move while we talk. I've got to get my stuff. We'd better hurry." We followed her across the creaky floor, to the stairs to the basement. Siren trotted ahead and down the stairs in front of us.

We clattered down the cement steps, past posters of Tour de France and Giro d'Italia racers. "That reminds me," I said. "A woman at the race said you should go pro. You could get paid to ride your bike and get out of here, and get away from your dad, and make enough money. Could you do that?"

"I've thought about that a lot—of trying to go pro—it's hard, but I think I could maybe do it. I wanted to wait for a few races this summer and kick some butt, and then maybe some bike companies would give me offers. It all takes time." The stairs at the bottom were narrow and wooden. The building was old, probably over a hundred years old, and down here the musty and bicycle-grease smells were overpowering. Allie turned the corner, still talking. "I had to wait until I had won enough money to leave. But when my dad got out of the slammer and came back to town, I ran out of time."

"Wait! How did you know your dad was out? Why didn't you tell us?"

"Long story. We gotta move. I'll try to explain in the car."

Cobwebs hung from some of the pipes overhead. The smell of greasy dust hung in the air. We turned a couple corners, passed some more yellowed, curling, ancient posters of European bicycle racers—I recognized Eddy Merckx and Fausto Coppi—and came into the end of a big room, lighted by a single dusty light bulb dangling from a cord. An air mattress lay on the floor covered with a quilt, blankets, and a pillow. A reading light glowed from a small table beside the mattress; one old kitchen chair, a bookcase with a table lamp, a hot plate, and a dorm-size refrigerator all crowded the corner, too. On one wall hung color posters of Lance Armstrong, Juli Furtado winning the Mountain Bike World Championship, and an aging poster of Missy Giove winning the downhill at Vail. Missy Giove had at least as many piercings as Allie.

"Welcome to my parlor, said the spider to the fly."

"Where'd you get all this stuff?"

"Discarded—from apartments up over the stores on this block. There's all sorts of shit in the storage room way in back." She motioned. "And Mike always had the refrigerator. He just let me bring it down here for now."

"So you've been here. Since Father Malcolm."

"Yeah. I went straight home to get Siren, a bag of clothes, and some posters, and came here. Stuff I could cram in my bag. Siren found me before I got home, though."

"We *knew* Mike knew something he wasn't telling us."

"Mike's cool. He told me you felt really bad not coming to meet me at four o'clock. So thanks for coming now. You probably shouldn't have, but we gotta go see Father Malcolm, so I'm glad you did. I just hope my dad's not waiting outside." Allie picked up a big hiking backpack with a sleeping bag tied on the top. She reached in the mini fridge and pulled out two bottles of Gatorade, which she stashed in the backpack. "Okay. I'm set." She turned toward her posters. "Bye, Lance. Julie. Missy. I'll call Mike for you later. Good bye, greasy dust bunnies. Guess I won't miss you." She shrugged into the backpack. "Let's go."

We started back up the stairs. Siren galloped up ahead of us.

Allie said, "You guys want to drive me and Siren and my bike to St. Peter after we leave the hospital?"

"Of course we could," Joe said. "But we're not ditching you in St. Peter. And if your dad is following us, wouldn't he follow us there, too? Scout told us to bring you home with us after the fireworks."

"Stay with us at Scout's, at least for tonight," I said. "Then we'll figure out what to do and we can take you somewhere else tomorrow. Okay?"

At the top of the stairs, Allie set down her bag. "The problem with the plan is that adults always seem to have to follow the rules. Afraid of breaking the law. The law says I'm under eighteen and if I leave home, I go to foster care, and believe me, I'm not doing that again."

"Allie," I said. "Just tell us quick. Why did you take off when we found Father Malcolm? I still don't get that. And when did you find out your dad was out of prison?"

"Let's *go*. I said I'd tell you in the car." She shouldered her giant backpack again.

I hooked Siren on his leash, Joe took Allie's bike, and Allie hauled her backpack. She locked the door and pulled it shut, moving like a giant turtle with a shell. We got her pack and Siren into the back seat. Allie kept looking around while we loaded her bike into the car-top bike rack. Then we all jumped in and took off.

We didn't speak for a couple blocks.

"Shit," Joe said, looking in his rearview mirror.

"What?" I whipped around.

"You said *shit,*" Allie said. She slid down into the back seat.

"It's him. He's following us!" Sure enough, the diesel pickup from after the race was cruising along behind us. A low-grade growl started rumbling from Siren's corner of the back seat.

"Shit again," Joe said. "I'm calling Scout."

"You were supposed to call before. I'll call," I said, grabbing the phone from him. "You drive."

Scout's phone rang and rang. "No answer. Should we drive around 'til we lose him?" I asked.

"Try again," Joe said. "I'll keep driving."

"Stay in town," Allie said. "Don't get on a highway where he can try to run us off the road."

I hit redial. No answer.

"Allie," Joe said, "Stay down. I suppose he already saw you, but it can't hurt."

"My bike's on top of the car, you moron."

Joe ignored that. "Tell us. What does all this have to do with Father Malcolm? What should we do? We can't exactly go to the hospital like this. Your dad'll catch us in no time."

I punched Scout's number in again. "Scout! Thank god. We've got Allie and her dog, but Cecil Baker is following us in his truck!"

Scout said, "Drive around for five minutes and park in front of the police station. I'll call the cops, and I'll be there in less than five. I'll meet you there. That should freak him out. It should keep him from trying something, and you can get away. Ask Allie what the conditions of her dad's parole are."

"What?" I looked over the back seat.

"I heard," said Allie. "He has to stay away from me." I repeated this into the phone.

"Enough info for me," said Scout. "He's breaking parole following you. Drive to the Cop Shop in five minutes. I'm calling the cops right now."

So we did. Scout's Land Rover idling there was the best thing I'd seen for a long time. The diesel pickup slowed behind us and stopped half a block back.

Scout swung himself out of his Land Rover, came over to Joe's car, and leaned in my window. Siren barked. "Shh, Siren," Allie said. Siren shushed.

Scout made a show of pulling his phone out of his pocket. He punched 911. "I hope this works. Otherwise, I'm going to look like a big fool. And I'm on probation, remember."

"I'm sorry, Scout," Allie said from her prone position in the back seat. "This is why I hid. I didn't want you guys to get involved. You're not going to look like a fool, I promise."

In thirty seconds, three cops came hustling out of the building. Cecil gunned his engine, spun out, and roared away in a cloud of diesel exhaust. Two police cars took off in the same direction.

"Allie," Scout said, "what did your dad do?"

"For starters, I'm positive he's the one who beat Father Malcolm up. As soon as I saw him in the woods, I knew my dad was back in town."

"What?" My stomach turned and I thought I'd lose my burgers and ice cream, digested as it was. Joe and I stared at each other and then at Allie.

Scout ran his fingers down his cheeks and chin. "You sure? And why would that be? And you can sit up. Your old man is nowhere in sight."

Allie sat up, one arm around Siren. "Father Malcolm is the one who turned my dad in."

We all looked at Allie. Scout said, "For...?"

Allie rubbed Siren's head. "Abuse. Sexual abuse."

We blew out our collective breaths. Scout eyed Allie for a long moment and nodded his head. "You're a brave one, young lady."

Joe reached over and squeezed my hand. "My God," he said.

"You swore again," I said.

"I think this calls for swear-worthy language."

"Okay, go!" Scout interrupted. "Go to the hospital now. I'll follow you up there to make sure Cecil Baker doesn't, and I'll ask the cops to send somebody up there, too, to keep an eye out the whole time. Go while you can.

Allie, you're staying with us tonight. I'll ask the cops for surveillance at our place, and I'll deal with the aunts."

"No, Scout," Allie said. "You've got little kids."

"No argument, Miss Allie Baker. You're staying. Oh, and here." He thrust a Tupperware container at her. "Leftover burger and potato salad from our picnic. When I told Susan and Janie what was going on, they were worried that you haven't eaten today. Humor them and eat it. Now get going."

"Thanks, Scout!"

So we went.

TWENTY-SEVEN

Finding Father Again

July 4, the day that lasts forever

While Allie devoured the burger, Siren sat beside her, head cocked, hoping for handouts. She fed him the last two big bites and he licked her face in thanks. "Yeah, I love you, too, Siren. Now settle down, please." After that, the loudest thing in the car besides maybe the pounding of our hearts was the sound of Siren panting. He stuck his head out the window frequently, tongue flapping like the official Fourth of July flag. Once he had to snap his head sideways to catch his tongue, as if he was afraid it would blow away if he lost control of it.

I still wanted to ask Allie a million questions, but it didn't seem like the time. Trying to absorb what she'd just told us was enough.

At the hospital, Scout pulled into the parking lot behind us. The second Siren couldn't see Allie, he sent up a howl. I grabbed his leash and got him out of the car. He wagged and smiled and licked my face. Gratitude.

Allie grinned. "He likes you."

I rubbed his ears.

Allie tied Siren to the bike rack near the front door of the hospital, and when we moved away from him, he set up a yowl that could wake the dead. "Siren," Allie said. "We don't have time to calm you down." She looked up at Joe and me. "See how he got his name?"

"Trouble's coming?" I said.

"Trouble's here," Allie said. "Too late for a warning this time, Siren. Calm down."

When Allie moved toward the hospital door, Siren set up a yowl again.

"I'll just stay with him for a while," Joe said. "You two go up."

Scout pulled up beside us. "Looks calm around here. Cop said someone's on the way. Don't be long. Just talk to him and head out, okay? I'll meet you at the fireworks. And—call. Remember to call."

"Thanks. Bye, Scout."

Joe sat down on the grass beside Siren. Allie rubbed Siren's head. "Thanks, Joe. Be right back, Siren."

Then she and I went inside.

The woman at the information desk frowned at us. "Visiting hours were over at nine."

"We got called," Allie said quickly. "That Father Malcolm is waking up, they said. Father Malcolm Dykstra. We need to see him."

"Room 3411."

"We know."

The elevator doors opened at third floor, intensive care.

The nurse at the desk looked up and her mouth fell open. It was Zia, the nurse Allie had knocked on her butt.

"You!" she said. She narrowed her eyes at Allie. "You be careful?"

"I promise. I'm really sorry about knocking you over that night."

Zia nodded. "I stay out of your way today. I wish you luck. I think is good luck that you are together again. Good, I think?"

"Yes!" I said and smiled at her. She smiled back.

At first, Father Malcolm's room looked just the same. Same tubes, same respirator, same breathing noise pulsing air in and out.

"Hi, Father," Allie said. "It's just me again."

A tall woman, with short dark hair and a white jacket, breezed in. Cheery but authoritative. All business. "Hi, I'm Dr. Rathburn. I've seen you here before," she said to Allie.

Allie nodded. "And this is Sadie."

"Father?" Dr. Rathburn leaned over the rails on his bed and put her hand on his arm. "Father? Allison is here to see you. And Sadie. Allie and Sadie. I think you want to talk with them."

"He doesn't know me," I said.

"Allison is here," the doctor repeated.

"It's me, Father," Allie leaned over him. "It's Allie."

This time, Father Malcolm's eyes fluttered, trying to open. Allie moved her head closer, into his line of sight.

"Father?" Allie asked. Her voice was un-Allie-like. Timid.

His eyes fixed open, then fell shut, then fluttered again. The fingers protruding from his cast moved slightly.

"Talk some more," Dr. Rathburn urged. "He can hear you."

"Father? It's Allie. Allie Baker. I came to see you. I brought my friend Sadie."

"Aaaa..." Father Malcolm said.

"Allie Baker," Allie said.

"Aaaalleeee."

"Yes!"

"Are...you..." He stopped and breathed three times. "O...kay?" The respirator and his chest rattled.

"I am. Are you gonna be okay?" She leaned even closer, careful not to touch him. "Father, you have to get well. You have to be okay," she said. "We need you."

"Allieeeee...I..." He stopped to breathe, tried to speak again, but it seemed to take too much effort.

"Father?" Allie said.

One corner of his mouth went up slightly. His whole face was still purple, his nose was still taped, and he was still attached to too many tubes, including the one pumping yellow fluid from his lower regions.

"Al...leeee..."

"Father!" Allie said. "Did my dad do this to you?"

Dr. Rathburn stepped over to the side of the bed.

His response was first just heavy breathing, but then Father Malcolm's head went up and down in a nod. A very slow, slight, but distinct nod. It took so much effort that his breathing became even louder. "Yessss...Al...leee..."

"Oh my God," Allie said. She put her hand on top of his. "I was right. I knew it."

Dr. Rathburn put her hand on Allie's shoulder. Allie straightened, stiffening at the touch. Dr. Rathburn said, "Allison. I'm going to go call the detective." And she disappeared.

Allie leaned over again. "Father. I'm so sorry. I'm so sorry. It's my fault."

Father Malcolm moved his head ever so slightly side to side. "No, Aaallleee. Not...not....your..."

Allie bit her lip and kept her hand on his.

"...fault," he finished. "You..." He breathed again, once, twice, three, four times. "Be...care...ful."

We stood for what felt like a long, long time, hoping for more, but he was lost again, unconscious, exhausted from this effort. He was somewhere inside the rise and fall of breathing, as if this tent of a man was reduced to a bellows made of skin and could do nothing more than force air in and out. In. Out.

Zia came in, her shiny, smiley self. "How's this priest? Did he talk to you?"

Allie said nothing, holding Father Malcolm's hand, staring at him.

"Yes," I said. "He did. He knows Allie."

"Good." Zia sad. "Very good. See? What I told you?"

"Dr. Rathbun just went to call the detective," I said. Zia hurried out the door.

Allie leaned her elbows on the bed rails and put her head in her hands. She said, "Sadie, would you go check if Joe and Siren are okay?"

"Allie, they should be fine. They—"

"Please? I have a bad feeling. Really bad."

I scampered down the stairs, two at a time, instead of taking the elevator.

Outside, Joe was sitting cross-legged and Siren lay curled up, sleeping with his nose on Joe's thigh. I breathed out. Siren jumped up and wagged.

"I think you have a friend," I said. I rubbed Siren's head. "You okay?" I asked Joe.

"Yeah. What's going on?"

"He woke up. Allie asked him if her dad did it, and he nodded *yes*."

"Holy crap."

Siren licked my hand and sat back down.

Then just as fast, he jumped to his feet again, snarling and barking toward the dark parking lot. I jumped back, afraid for my fingers. Joe jumped up and held tight to Siren's leash. "Siren! What's wrong?"

Siren's snarling mouth was so close to us, we could feel his hot stinky breath.

"Siren, what is it?"

Siren snarled a growl that made me shudder. His hackles were up and he barked into the darkness.

"This gives me the creeps," Joe said.

"Do you think he's out there?"

Joe shrugged. "He is, somewhere. I sure hope not here."

A Mankato police car eased around the corner. Out stepped Officer Rankin.

Siren barked.

"Siren, don't you like cops?" asked Joe.

Siren's rumbly growl subsided as Officer Rankin approached. "Whoa there." Rankin extended the back of his hand to Siren. Siren sniffed and then stood still, letting Rankin touch him.

Rankin nodded to us. "Sadie, Joe. Allison upstairs? The doctor called me."

We nodded, and Rankin went inside.

I smoothed Siren's hackles. He looked up at me. Panting, still nervous, but calmer. He licked my face. Nervous, quick, wet licks.

"It's a quarter to ten," Joe said. "Almost time for fireworks."

"Fireworks? I said. "Aren't fireworks for people who need to create excitement in their lives? I keep forgetting this is the Fourth of July." It was the longest day on earth, hands down. It was an eternity ago that we rode a bike race.

TWENTY-EIGHT

Allie, Father Malcolm, and Cecil Baker

Still the Fourth of July

What seemed a long time later, the hospital door opened.

Siren leapt up and charged so fast, he jerked Joe right over. Allie stepped toward us, and Siren whirled and leapt at the end of the leash. She knelt beside him and wrapped her arms around him. He licked her face and wagged a million miles an hour. His tongue lolled out so far he could have stepped on it. She'd been gone maybe all of half an hour, and this was his greeting. She buried her face in his neck.

When she looked up at us, her face was the same color it had been when we found Father Malcolm in the ravine. "He's dead. Father Malcolm."

She sat down on the grass. Siren put his front paws and nose in her lap. "They're moving him, and Dr. Rathburn said we can come up then and say a final good-bye."

"Holy crap. That filthy, rotten bastard," Joe muttered.

"Dr. Rathburn?" I said.

"No. Allie's dad. Father Malcolm is dead. If Allie's dad did this, he *killed* the priest."

"It's my fault," Allie said, half-muffled against Siren's head. "He's dead because of me."

"Allie," I said, "that's bullshit."

Allie didn't look up.

"He's dead," Joe said, "and it's nobody's fault but the guy who did this to him."

Allie looked at me with the saddest eyes I've ever seen. "My dad," she said, "is a murderer. A murderer. My *dad* is a murderer. You can tell that to your fancy archeologist parents and see if they let you hang out with me. Another reason for me to disappear. Nobody should hang out with me. Look what happens."

"Sadie's right," Joe said. "That's bullshit."

Allie bit her lip.

"Stuff happens," Joe went on. "My brother died, and I blamed myself, and maybe I could have stopped him, but I couldn't know—didn't know—and none of that makes it my fault. This isn't your fault at all, Allie."

We were quiet again.

"Allie." I sat cross-legged beside her and rubbed Siren's ribs. He looked at me and then put his nose back on Allie's thigh. "I get why you took off when you knew your dad was back—when you knew your dad did this. I get why you needed to hide from him. But I still don't understand why you hid from us."

Allie stroked Siren's ear and said nothing.

"Allie. We need to know. Talk. Please."

Allie bit her lip, hard, then said, "I told you that Father Malcolm turned my dad in."

"Yeah, so? That doesn't make you responsible. Or explain why you hid."

"I told Father Malcolm what my dad was doing. In fact, Father Malcolm is the *only* one I ever told. And look what it got him. It's what happens to somebody who knows what my dad really is."

Joe leaned in toward Allie. "Look, Allie. Father Malcolm isn't dead because you talked to him. Father Malcolm is dead because somebody who's a low-down dirty horrible bastard, who is a despicable human being, beat him to death. If that's your dad, I'm sorry. But it doesn't have anything to do with you telling someone the truth."

Allie looked up and shrugged. "It does. This happened to Father Malcolm because he knew too much. That's why I hid from you guys. So you wouldn't know too much … "

Joe and I looked at each other. Maybe this was being in love. When you could say volumes with just your eyes. We both knew we could run, shut the door on this, be done, gone, and we both knew it was the last thing we would do.

"Allie," I said, "too late. You're my friend. Our friend. This is what friends do. They take shit for each other.

They stick together. You're not getting rid of us. We're here—" I smiled—"to *walk through the chicken* with you."

She looked up. "I get it. I think. Dad never let me have friends much."

"Of course not. Friends talk. If you had a friend, you might have told somebody else what was going on. So talk." I faced Allie.

She looked at us miserably.

Joe got to his feet. "Want me to take Siren for a walk? So you can talk to Sadie without me?"

Allie shook her head and rubbed Siren's front leg. "No, thanks. I want Siren here. And you might as well hear, too, Joe. Sit down."

Joe sat back down.

❌❌

So Allie talked.

"When I was almost twelve, I told him—Father Malcolm—in confession. My dad made me go to CCD and to confession. He believed in it like some sort of holy whitewash. If you go to confession, it will take care of rest of your sins or the shit in your life or something." She stroked Siren's ears.

"Yeah? And?"

"So I told Father Malcolm that Dad used to get my mom drugged or passed out drunk to get her out of the way. He dealt drugs, too, so there was always something around. Then he'd come to my room. First he just touched me. Then more and more, and then he forced himself on me... like at least once a week. Started when I was nine. The first time, I thought he'd split me in two."

We were silent, shocked.

"And Siren tried to tear him apart 'cause he knew Dad was hurting me and I was trying to get away," Allie continued. "Dad kicked Siren—broke his ribs once, after Siren attacked him. I grabbed Siren and lay on top of him, and wouldn't let go, and I was crying and screaming that Dad would have to shoot me to get Siren and I didn't care if he did. Shoot me, I mean. I wanted to just die."

Siren looked up into Allie's face, panting a smile, every time she said his name.

"After that, Dad used to tie Siren up outside. Usually he had to drug him—put drugs in some meat—so he wouldn't go crazy tied up away from me when he knew I was in trouble." Allie ran her hand down Siren's ribs. She didn't look up.

"If I made noise, he put a pillow over my mouth so no one would hear me scream or cry. I thought I was gonna suffocate, so I quit crying. Instead, I shut down. He didn't let me have friends, so I closed off the world."

Allie pulled her free knee—the one not under Siren's head—up to her chest and held it in her elbow, her face buried in it. I could hardly hear her. I barely breathed. And then, I saw a tear. Allie, tough girl, AllieCat, always-land-rubber-side-down-or-on-her-feet AllieCat was crying. She sniffed and wiped her nose on her knee.

"I only cried one other time after that. Ever." She glanced up at me, wiped her face with the back of her hand. "Until now." She grinned through the tears.

I nodded. I reached out and put my hand on her knee.

"Afterwards, he'd sort of wake up, like he couldn't help himself when he did it, and then he'd come to his senses, and feel bad, and make me food to try to make it up. Usually spaghetti, and he makes the best spaghetti in the world. Then there were leftovers the next day if Mom was too drunk to cook.

"Dad used to tell me that if I told anybody what he did, it would kill my mom, and he would have to go away and I'd be all alone. And nobody would make me food. I believed him. And in a warped way, he was right.

"You know what's crazy? I thought God knew everything, so he already knew what my dad was doing, so if I told Father Malcolm, it was nothing new under the sun for God. And if God already wasn't doing anything about it, what the hell could Father Malcolm do? So nothing would happen.

"Boy was I wrong.

"When I came out of the confessional that time, Father Malcolm was crying, too. The cops went straight to our trailer while Mom was waiting outside the church to pick me up, and they arrested Dad right then and there. They had a search warrant, and they found some drugs, too. The social worker came and took me to a foster home.

"Father Malcolm came to see me the next day at the foster home, and I told him God had only screwed things up. He hadn't fixed anything and Dad was right—now I was all alone. But Father Malcolm took me to A-1 that day and got me a bike. I loved that bike. It was a blue Giant mountain bike. I rode it and rode it and never quit."

She laughed a half laugh, and she looked at both of us. "Some things pay off, I guess. I got faster and faster. And I knew how to change a tire and fix the chain before I was thirteen. That was the nicest thing anybody ever did for me, I guess. After my dad got sent to prison, I moved back home with Mom. And now I had a bike." She grinned and rubbed her eyes with the heels of her hands.

"So," she continued, "when I saw Father Malcolm beat up, I was sure my dad was out of prison. I knew he would go after him 'cause he would blame him for getting sent away. Who else would beat up a priest—a really good priest—in the middle of the woods?"

"Wow," I said.

"I knew he'd blame me, too, and he'd never leave me alone unless I disappeared. And you couldn't know where I was either, in case he found you."

I reached over to rub Siren's ears. He licked my hand. Then he turned, ears up, toward the hospital door.

Zia stepped out, looked up and down the sidewalk, and saw us. "There you are. I look and look everywhere for you. Here, finally, you are. Come in now. Say good-bye to the priest."

Joe jumped up and then reached out two hands to pull us both to our feet. I took his hand, but Allie stood up on her own.

"We won't be too long," Allie said. "Siren, will you stay put if we tie you up so Joe can come in?" She tied his leash to the bike rack, triple knotting it, and kissed his nose. "We'll be right back."

So we followed her inside. Siren whimpered, but he didn't howl.

We took the elevator, and during the silent ride, I thought about my mom in Egypt. I thought about how mad I'd been at her getting to go do research for the summer, and how mad I'd been at them for getting divorced. And I felt about as big as a speck of dust.

Dr. Rathburn met us at the door and said, "I don't know what you believe about dying, but I suppose there's some comfort in the idea that, if what the Father believed is true, he's in a better place and out of pain."

"I wish I believed that," Allie said. "But I kinda doubt it. God hasn't been too good at taking care of stuff as far as I can tell."

The doctor gave Allie a sad smile and led us through a door. "Here he is. I'm very sorry about this. Take as much time as you need."

The room was tiny and looked sterile. A sheet covered Father Malcolm's face. The body's face. Allie lifted it. It reminded me of her lifting the blue tarp off him, only much slower, and much more gently. My eyes met Joe's. I could tell he thinking about his brother.

Father Malcolm didn't look that different than he had in the woods. Just without all the blood and without the raspy breathing.

Joe made a choking sound, like retching. "I gotta go," he said. He squeezed my hand and scooted out the door. I thought I should follow him. I was torn between staying and going. I needed to be both places, with Allie and with Joe. A good girlfriend should go. But I hadn't been around for Allie lately. I ached to give Joe a hug.

I stayed with Allie.

Allie stood, stoic, beside the dead man. The first time I ever saw this guy was as the injured victim of a beating, never as a whole man, never as a priest. Then he was a mess of wounded flesh, and now he was dead flesh. I wished I'd met him before he got beaten to a pulp. This priest was the only man who was really, really good to Allie in her early life, and he was gone. Her dad had a way of taking everything good away from her.

As I looked at Father Malcolm Dykstra, I wondered if he had relatives somewhere, brothers or sisters or even ancient parents. Or if he was alone in the world except for God and the church. And of course, the nuns.

I was connected to him because of how we found him in the woods, because of waiting by his messed-up body for the ambulance, and now, now I was connected because I was here at the hospital while he died. I'd never been around somebody dying before. I thought about the Catholic mass and death and souls departing, and I stared hard at this body that had been breathing twenty minutes ago, and still would be if it weren't for Cecil Baker.

Father Malcolm was the same tent of loose skin that he was twenty minutes ago, but now, there was no air going in and out. The system just stopped working. Like maybe talking wore out the last shred of life energy he had. Somehow, I'd always thought that if there was a God at all, then death would be spiritual, otherworldly, angelic or something. But it wasn't, even for a priest. There sure weren't any angels around when we were in his room. Death just put the brakes on his breathing and his heartbeat, stopping the parts that were still working. Just stopping. Twenty minutes ago his body was doing something, and now it wasn't. Father Malcolm Dykstra just stopped being alive.

I stood in awe, waiting for Allie to be done. Allie didn't cry. She stood there and stood there, and finally, she reached out and patted Father's hand. "I'm sorry, Father. Thanks for everything. I'm so sorry."

TWENTY-NINE

Fireworks

The never-ending Fourth of July

I followed Allie down the stairs, saying nothing. She slid her hand along the railing and stepped with more weight in each footfall than I thought possible for her lithe body.

"Allie!" As we stepped into the lobby, Joe met us, his face full of horror. "Siren's gone."

"Gone? You sure? Shit!" She tore past him and would have shoved him out of the way except that he backed up against the wall to let her through. Then Joe and I were on her heels.

"Siren!" Allie screamed. "Siren!" Siren had been sitting by the bike rack when we last saw him. Now the leash dangled where Allie had so carefully triple-knotted it. "Did he chew through it?" She dashed over, bent, and picked up the end of the leash. It was cut clean through— a sharp, clear cut—nothing any dog's teeth could manage.

"Fuck!" Allie grabbed her hair and bent over like she was about to throw up. "He fucking *took* Siren. God, he'll stoop lower than I even thought. Ohmygod, I shouldn't have left him alone! Why did I do that? I should have known! Sadie, what's wrong with me! Ohmygod!"

"How could you have guessed *that*?" I said. "You positive it was your dad?"

"YES!" She whirled on me like it was my fault, but I didn't blame her. "Siren *never* lets anybody touch him or his leash unless I'm around. So somebody had to drug him o—or kill him—to take him like this. My dad is the only asshole I know mean enough to do either one, and he's the *only* person who would want to."

I said, "Like he was the only one who would beat up a priest."

"You got it. Goddam! I know my dad well enough—I can't believe I left Siren alone!"

Joe blew his breath out in a near whistle. "So let's go get him."

My stomach wrenched a flip at the thought of Cecil Baker, but I nodded.

"No," Allie said. "No, you guys don't have to do this. I'll go."

"Look, Allie Baker," Joe said, whirling on her. "You harassed me into quitting smoking. You hauled our asses around the countryside and kicked our butts up so many hills that we actually raced okay this morning. That was today, wasn't it?" His jaw was tense and I could see a vein in his neck pulsing. "It's so long ago, I hardly remember, but yeah. And yeah, your old man is the biggest pain-in-the-ass baddass son-of-a-bitch I've ever met, but we're your *friends*. You're stuck with us, and you are *not* doing this alone. Come on. Get in my car."

"Wow," Allie said, "I guess you mean it. Okay, then." We all trotted to the trusty orange-red Grand Am. "You should call Scout. Is that cop still upstairs?"

"No, he left when I was on my way downstairs," Joe said.

Joe unlocked the car, and Allie stepped up onto the bottom of the door frame to unlock her bike.

"Why don't I go first on my bike and sort of catch Dad off guard, and then you can come in with the cavalry in a couple minutes. Get Scout, and maybe one of the cops. Okay?"

"Holy crap," Joe said, ripping a note out from under his windshield wiper. "Look."

"Allison" was scrawled across the front. Joe held it out to Allie.

She jumped down, whipped it open and read, *"Your dad sent us to get your flea-bitten dog. He said if you want to see him alive again, you better come home pronto."*

"Fuck him! Fuck them!" She crumpled the note, threw it down, and stepped back up to her bike. "I don't believe this shit! Look! My tires are flat! The son-of-a-bitches slashed my tires!" She jumped back down again. "I guess we're all going together. That okay, Joe?"

"Get in!"

Allie jumped in the back seat. "Joe, drive fast, okay? I'm so scared for Siren."

I grabbed the crumpled note off the pavement, just in case we needed to show it to a cop. I jumped into the front seat.

Joe slipped the Grand Am into reverse, then slammed it into drive and we peeled out of the parking lot.

"Look. There's the last of the fireworks finale," I said, fastening my seat belt and pointing to the MSU campus.

"Siren hates fireworks," Allie said. "I hope he can't hear them. Just drive, Joe, okay? Can Sadie use your phone to call Scout? And 911? Again?"

Joe handed me his phone and steered down the street, going way over the speed limit. I dialed Scout. While his phone rang, I rolled my window all the way down to let the night air rush over my face. It was still almost as hot as it had been during the race. *Like riding through hell.*

Joe's radio crackled faintly, the Beatles song "Lucy in the Sky with Diamonds," while bursts of color exploded in the finale over our heads and I waited for Scout to answer his phone.

Allie groaned and slouched in the back seat. "Oh, poor Siren."

I hung up and dialed again. "Come on, Scout, come on. Answer the—Hi! Oh, I'm so glad you answered!" I gave him the super-fast run-down. "So we need you to meet us at Allie's. When I get off the phone, I'm calling the cops to come, too ... Allie, where do you live?"

"The LeHillier trailer court. That shit hole."

"Scout wants an address—your house number."

I relayed the information to Uncle Scout. "Now," I added. "We need you now. Faster than is humanly possible, please."

I punched 9-1-1.

"Yeah. Is Rankin there? Officer Kate?...Well, tell somebody to get to 437 Sandstone Lane in LeHillier *now*. This is Sadie Lester..." And I told the dispatch officer as much as I could in a hurry. "Hurry, please. This is the guy that killed Father Malcolm."

Joe followed Allie's directions and we turned down the gravel road toward the trailer park. Smaller fireworks popped in the sky over us, illegal blossoms of color.

"Go this way." Allie pointed toward the dumpster cemetery route. "It's the back way, and you'll come out behind our place. It might be less obvious." We were all for being less obvious, so we went the way she was pointing.

We bumped down the dirt road, which was grassy in spots, and we drove through the parting of the Red Sea, watching both sides as if expecting somebody to jump out at us from one of the rusty dead dumpsters. Joe turned the corner, which cut through a short section of the junk woods and came out in the trailer court.

He turned. The car hit two huge ruts and the bottom hit dirt with a sickening THUNK, but the car chugged on past, the bottom scraping every now and then through the ruts.

Allie directed us again, this time to the road behind her trailer. "Here," she said. "Let me out. I'm gonna sneak around and see if Siren's around front."

"You nuts?" Joe said. "You're not doing that alone."

"Joe," I said, "I wish Scout was already here."

"I know," he said. "He should be soon."

We parked. Allie pulled something long and skinny from her backpack and stuck it in her back pocket, but I couldn't see what it was in the dark.

We trotted through the back side of Allie's block of trailers. "Good thing," Joe puffed quietly, "that I quit smokin'."

"Shh now," Allie warned.

The place was silent, like a big sleeping pack of dangerous dogs. The fireworks popping behind us seemed like something from some other world. Here, there were no trees. There were trailers, trashed vehicles, usable vehicles, four-wheelers, and piles of junk to hide behind. Otherwise, we were out in the open.

We came to the back of Allie's place, my heart hammering and sweat streaming down my back. I'd forgotten how tired I was. We crept through dusty weeds toward the side of her trailer. Back here, there were discarded tires, but they were in neat piles. Probably Allie's work, I figured.

We turned the corner. On the side, a mass of sunflowers bobbed their heads, bowed in the dark. Allie motioned toward them. "In honor of the Tour de France," she whispered. "I plant them every year. Wait! Listen."

She stopped, frozen, held her hand up to stop me. I could hear it too. A very faint whimpering, the sound of a dog unable to make a sound but trying with everything he was worth.

Allie stepped to the front edge of the trailer, peeked around, and yanked herself back. She looked at us, eyes wild, and motioned to the front of the trailer. "He's there," she mouthed. "Dad has Siren. And a gun." She held her hand to mime a pistol, a fist with pointer finger out and thumb up.

My heart was hammering. I was sure Joe and Allie and Cecil Baker himself could hear it, it was so loud. My throat wasn't working.

"Wait here," she mouthed at us. She whistled low, and we could hear a scrambling, scuffling, as Siren tried to respond to Allie's whistle. The sound that wasn't a whimper became more desperate to be one.

"Allison?" Cecil said. "Allison, I know you're there. I knew you'd come. Come to Daddy."

Allie breathed out, deep. She looked back at us, and motioned us to stay where we were. She put her hand over her mouth, then dropped it, ran her hand through her hair, put her shoulders back, and stepped between the house and the four-wheeler ATV I'd seen Cecil riding.

"Dad, I came—what's wrong with Siren?"

"Nothing's wrong. He's just sleepy is all. Allison, come to Daddy. Come here, baby."

"Dad, what did you do to him?"

"I didn't do anything to him. I just put the muzzle on him."

"What did you have *them* do to him, then, the two assholes you sent?"

"Aren't you glad to see your daddy?"

I dropped flat on the ground and slid behind the four-wheeler, creeping forward just until I could see Allie and Cecil from underneath it. Squatted beside Siren, Cecil had a steel choke chain around the dog's neck and a muzzle over his mouth. Siren had to be drugged, because his eyes were rolling and he was swaying as if he were drunk. Cecil was holding a pistol.

Allie moved toward Siren and Cecil stood up, letting Siren flop onto his side.

Joe hit the ground beside me, his hip and leg against mine. He grabbed my hand.

Cecil stuffed the gun into the back of his jeans and reached out to Allie. "Come to Daddy, baby."

"Dad, what's wrong with him? How much—what—did they give him!?"

"They gave him a tranquilizer to get him. And then when he got here, he was freaked out from the fireworks. So I put a little OxyContin in some meat," Cecil said. "Maybe a bit much, but he'll be okay. You know how he gets and sometimes he won't let me get close to him otherwise. Come and give your daddy a hug." Cecil grabbed Allie's arm and pulled her against him. I imagined that chest as hard as rawhide.

Allie's arms hung at her sides. "You're not supposed to be here. Or anywhere near me. You're breaking parole."

"I had to see you, baby. You know that. Come on inside, though, just in case."

"Dad, no. I have to help Siren first. Something's really wrong with him."

Even in his drugged state, Siren swiped a paw at the muzzle, trying to get it off.

"Give your daddy a hug first."

Allie lifted doll-like arms, and put them around her father's back. I couldn't believe those sinewy arms of hers could move with such stiffness.

Siren's body spasmed violently.

"Dad! I have to get that muzzle off him. He can't breathe. It's too hot. He needs to pant." She tore herself from her father's arms and dropped to her knees beside Siren.

"Leave the damn muzzle on. You know he bites."

"He can't breathe! He could die." Allie fumbled with the buckle.

Joe poked me in the ribs. When I looked at him, he jerked his head to the left. There was Scout, out of sight, plastered as much as a man his size could be, around the corner of the trailer. He held his finger to his lips and then pointed across the yard and dirt road. Behind the Bakers' neighbors' trashed car and pile of anti-freeze cans and tires, overgrown with weeds, I could see Thomas, on his knees, a black powder rifle drawn and pointed straight at Cecil.

We had the cavalry! Or the infantry, I guess it was. But we didn't have Allie, and we didn't have Siren.

Allie kissed Siren's head and worked frantically to unbuckle the muzzle.

Cecil yanked Allie by one arm and said, "Leave the dog be. He'll be fine. He'll come out of it in an hour or so. I *said*, get in the house."

"He'll *die* if you leave him here with the muzzle on."

"He won't *die*. I *said*, get in the house. Before the cops come. You love the damn dog more than your daddy?"

"It's too hot and he's drugged. He can't get enough air. He *has* to pant."

"Leave the muzzle on so he won't bite when he wakes up. Now get in the damn house," Cecil said through his teeth. "Leave him be." They were indeed father and daughter.

"I'm getting this off him *first*!" Allie's voice rose higher and higher.

"Get … in … the—"

"No! Not 'til—"

Siren thrashed violently.

"He's having a seizure or something!" This time Allie jerked away and got the buckle open, ripped the muzzle off Siren, but I could see the gray body twitching violently anyway, legs flailing. Siren lurched, legs stiff, and the spasms stopped. Then he went limp.

"No! No! Siren! Siren! Look at me, Siren!"

Cecil stood, staring down. Allie took Siren's head in her hands. "Siren! Siren!" She touched his eyelid and got no response. She shook him. She leaned her head down to Siren's chest and held it there for a moment. "No. No. Nooooo! Nooooo!" She sat up, still holding his head.

"He's dead." She looked up at her father. "You."

Her voice was the same, level, deadly emotionless voice her father could use. "You. You killed my dog."

She laid Siren's head gently on the ground and rose to her feet. "You *killed* my dog! You *killed* Siren!"

Allie's voice rose to a roar, and as quick as she'd grabbed the pool ball and hurled it at the rednecks, she whipped her bike pump from her back pocket and charged her father. She swung with all the might that planted that cue ball into the Last Chance paneling, and with all the might that could beat the pants off anybody climbing a hill on a bike, and with all her might, she brought her tire pump against her father's face with a sickening crack.

"You killed Siren, and you killed Father Malcolm, and you don't get to take *anything more* away from me! You hear?"

Cecil staggered, grabbed at his head and pulled the gun from his jeans. "Stop, Allie. Baby. Stop." He was bleeding from the eye, and the pump opened a cut from his eye down his cheek. His nose wasn't straight anymore, and trickled blood. Allie swung again, at his gun hand, connecting with the knuckles wrapped around the gun, and the gun went off in the air, the pistol's crack blasting a hole into the trailer just below the roof. Smoke and debris flew. Allie swung again, both hands, like she had a bat, cracking the bike pump into his jaw, fast as lightning, and again at his gun hand.

Then Cecil's other arm snaked out and captured her against him, by the neck, trying to squeeze off her windpipe. "Stop it, you wildcat."

I didn't remember moving, but I was on my feet, moving towards Allie.

"Sadie! No!" Thomas's voice barked from the shadows. "Cecil, let her go. Get your goddam hands up. Right now."

In front of me, Cecil waved his pistol toward the voice, saw me, and pointed the gun at me. Allie went crazy, fighting like a wildcat.

Thomas stepped out of the shadows, and Cecil fired in Thomas' direction.

Another gunshot cracked in my eardrums. Cecil lurched forward, still holding Allie.

A dark spot bloomed on Cecil's shoulder. He tried to aim his pistol at Thomas, but his arm wasn't working right, and the pistol went off far in front of Thomas's feet.

Then Cecil waved the gun in my direction, and Scout moved around me faster than he'd moved on Memorial Day, faster than anything that big should be able move.

Cecil had a moment of confusion, riddled with pain, trying to aim again and facing a black-powder rifle on one side and a giant charging him on the other. He decided to shoot at the giant Scout, who was about to eclipse the moon in the sky as he tackled him.

The gun went off at Scout as all three of them—Scout, Cecil, and Allie—hit the ground. The pistol flew out of Cecil's hand.

Scout held him down. Thomas came thundering over, and the muzzle of the black-powder rifle, in Thomas's hands, was against Cecil's temple. "Move again," Thomas said, "and I'll blow your head off. And I'd love to get to do it, so I'm hopin' you move. Scout, you alive?"

Scout grunted.

Allie scrambled out from the pile over to Siren. Her wail was almost as loud as the gunshot. She sank to her knees and took Siren's head in her lap, rocking back and forth in the dirt and weeds, rocking and rocking.

She didn't even look over her shoulder when she finally could speak enough to ask, "Scout, did he shoot you?"

"Yup," Scout said.

"You going to be okay?"

"Flesh wound," he said. "Plenty of it here to hit, too. He couldn't have missed." He was trying to laugh, but his voice was pinched with pain.

The mobile home door opened with a tinny squeak. A woman in a wrinkled aqua bathrobe and dark circles around her eyes leaned in the doorway. She peered into the dim yardlight and shielded her eyes with a pale, bony hand. "Wha—What was that?" she said. "Cecil? Honey? I heard guns." Her black hair was streaked with gray and hung in a messy ponytail. "Allison? Is that you, honey? What happened?"

She staggered out onto the top step, a skeleton in an bathrobe, and saw Scout's body still pinning Cecil to the ground, Thomas standing over them both with a gun to her husband's head, and she started screaming. "Who— Who are you? What are you doing to my husband? Did you shoot him?!" Then she let loose a full-bodied scream. "Cecil! Ohmygod, Cecil!"

"Mom!" Allie screamed right back, and then her voice got quiet. "Mom. Dad started it." She kept rocking Siren. Without looking up, she said, "Meet my mother."

✖✖

Sirens wailed down the gravel street, coming toward us. I was getting used to that sound. And it was nothing new in LeHillier.

THIRTY

Siren

July 4, continued

After the police hauled Cecil away in one ambulance and Scout in another, Allie's mom got hauled to detox.

We went to the hospital, where Officer Rankin and another detective talked to us for over an hour.

✖✖

The pistol shell had lodged against Scout's collarbone, so they took him in for emergency surgery to remove it. He'd have to stay at Immanuel-St. Joe's for a couple days.

Cecil had a deep flesh wound where the bullet from Thomas's black-powder rifle had grazed his upper arm. "I'm a better shot than I thought," Thomas said. "Couldn't have asked to hit him in a better spot. Good thing Cecil didn't know I can only load one bullet at a time. When I held the gun to his head, it was empty."

But the wound meant Cecil was on lock-down in the hospital.

We brought Allie home with us from the police station in Thomas's extended-cab pickup. I led her down to my cedar closet and she curled into a ball next to me on the roll-out bed. I wanted to put my hand on her shoulder, but I didn't dare. I lay there, listening to her breathe.

July 5

Allie decided to bury Siren in the junk woods where we found Father Malcolm. We'd wrapped him in a sheet and left him in the garage overnight. Peapod wanted to get into the garage in the worst way, but I didn't let him in. First thing in the morning, we went out to bury Siren. It was too hot to wait even one day, so we couldn't wait for Scout.

Allie carried Siren herself. She wrapped him in her quilt from the bike shop. He was heavy, and when we'd brought him to Scout's, he was like a rag doll. Now he was stiff and unwieldy, but she refused to let any of us carry him. We followed her, in an odd funeral procession: Allie with her awkward bundle of Siren; Peapod right behind her, sniffing at Siren; then me and Joe, each bearing a shovel; Megan, who insisted on helping; and Timmy, Stevie, and Thomas with three shovels.

Allie laid Siren down by where we were going to dig. Peapod sniffed him all over, pawed at him, trying to wake him up, whined, and lay down right next to Siren's body like they were two puppies from the same litter. Peapod didn't budge or quit whimpering the whole time the four of us took turns digging.

Buzzards circled above us, three of them, like graceful two-toned kites. When we were finally done, we had a five-foot-deep grave so nobody would ever dig him up.

Only then, we looked up at the buzzards. "Damn things," Thomas said, mopping his face with his hanky. "They're pretty from down here."

"Funny, isn't it," I said, "that anything so ugly up close can be glorious from way down here?"

"Hope heaven isn't like that," Joe said. He looked at me. "If there is one."

"Ha," Thomas says. "I wouldn't put my bets on it, either way."

Allie threw down her shovel and screamed toward the sky, "You can't have him! You bastard buzzards! Go away! You *can't* have him!"

She scooped Siren up, climbed down into the grave, laid him down, snug in the quilt. She patted his head and his haunches one last time, bent over to kiss his nose, covered his nose with the quilt, and then climbed out of the hole.

Thomas said, "Allie, sorry this is so hard." I could tell he would have hugged her if he thought she'd let him, but it was obvious that he remembered the last time he tried to touch her. "It sucks to lose such a good friend."

Allie stared down into the hole. "Two friends in one day. Why is it the good ones get killed and the ones who do the hurting just keep on going?"

"I'll second that question," Joe said.

"No rhyme or reason that I can figure," Thomas said.

"Siren was the best dog in the world," Allie said. She reached out and touched Peapod's head. "No offense, buddy."

"They say," Thomas said, "that a good life is six dogs long. We always outlive our good dogs."

"Maybe this is the price I gotta pay for having a great dog in my life for almost seven years."

When we started dropping shovelfuls of dirt on top of his body, Peapod watched, then sat up and started to howl. It was eerie. We stopped and stood, shovels poised, watching him howl. Peapod stopped the racket and looked at each of us—first me, then Joe, then Thomas. Then he got up and nosed Allie's hand and whimpered. She sat down and wrapped her arms around him, buried her nose in his neck.

We waited. Finally, Allie got to her feet and threw in another shovelful of dirt. We joined her, and Peapod started howling again and howled until we were done filling in the dirt and piling stones on top. We piled so many rocks on top that it would take a bulldozer to move them. Peapod howled the whole time.

When we finished, Peapod went over to Allie, who let him lick the tears off her face.

"This is good," she said. "Peapod can visit him, and his ghost can chase rabbits and ground squirrels, and maybe keep out some of the morons who dump their junk in here."

"That would be a big job, even for a ghost dog," Thomas said.

All four of us walked back up the hill together, carrying our shovels. Peapod walked between Allie and me.

"You cried again," I said, wiping my own tears.

"Yup," she said. "You know, Sadie, this was the second time in twenty-four hours."

I nodded. "I know. But you barely even cried last night."

"Sometimes I'm too mad to cry."

"Sometimes it's good to cry." I reached over and squeezed her hand. She didn't pull away. She squeezed back.

Even more amazing, while we were walking, Joe reached over and put his arm around her shoulder. I expected her to pull away, but she didn't. She let him almost hug her, and she almost hugged him back. And then she wiped snot on her T-shirt sleeve.

THIRTY-ONE

Allie and Me

July 5, continued

After Siren's funeral, Allie and I went for a walk down by the river with Peapod.

We stopped and watched the sunlight dapple the water. We walked until we saw the chain-saw sign, water-logged off its nails, at the bottom of the tree.

"What a moron," Allie said, shaking her head. "Hey, Sadie?"

"Hmm?"

"Thanks." She looked at me, held my gaze. "For everything."

She stepped close and touched my shoulder. All I could think about was Joe asking me if she was a lesbian. Then she let me hug her. She hugged back and started to sob, slowly at first, and then harder and harder. I let her cry.

I felt like I was distant from myself, watching this happen. I felt too young to be doing this much comforting, with death all around. This must be what it's like in a war zone, I thought.

Then she kissed my cheek. I didn't kiss back.

"Too bad you're not into girls," Allie whispered. "I really, really like you."

I pulled back a little. She moved back a half step, but still held me. I could see in her face that she was scared she'd gone too far.

"Allie, I really, really like you, too. But not that way."

"I know. Sorry." She dropped her arms.

"No, no. It's okay." I grabbed both her hands. "You don't have to be sorry. You're the coolest girl I think I've ever met. If I was into girls, I would be into you! I told you before, most of the summer I've just wanted to *be* you."

"Ha! That's a good one. Not anymore, I bet. Who'd want to be me now?"

I grinned. "Well, it sure is more complicated than I thought before."

"That's a nice way to say my life is all fucked up."

And we smiled at each other, a big deep smile. And I reached out and pulled her into another long hug. And she hugged back.

✖✖

That night, Allie camped out with me in CCC again. For a while, I felt weird about sleeping in the same bed with a lesbian, and I wondered if she would hit on me when she was half-asleep. I mean, I wouldn't sleep in the same bed with a guy. But when I opened my eyes in the morning and she was still curled in a tight little ball on the other side of the double bed, I felt bad for even thinking it. Allie was Allie, and she didn't want to screw up our friendship either.

July 6

The next morning, she went back to her baking job in North Mankato, and I went back to the Blue Ox, blending into the world of red checks and twenty-four-ounce steaks.

Barb was cooking. "So," she said when I handed her an order, "what've you been up to? You gotta tell me why you needed an extra day off. Or did you have a boring Fourth of July like I did?"

I laughed. I didn't know where to start, so I said, "It wasn't boring, that's for sure. I got third in my mountain bike race."

"Way to go." She grinned at me.

"Oh, and the priest died. And Allie's dog died. And her dad got out of prison and got arrested again. And Thomas shot Allie's dad. And Joe kissed me." The least important detail of the day, it seemed now, but it was probably the one Barb would be most interested in. She stood there with her mouth open, staring at me.

I just headed for my first table and let her wonder.

Today: Staying Alive

July 8

Cecil Baker had his preliminary hearing on Friday. He's in custody, held without bail. He pleaded not guilty, of course, but the evidence was overwhelming against him. The trial is set for November. Joe and I will have to testify, along with Allie, of course, and Thomas, Scout, and Dr. Rathburn, so Joe will come back from Phoenix and I'll have to come down from Minnetonka for it. The lawyer said he has *no* idea how long the trial will last. At least I'll get to see Joe in November.

No charges were filed against Thomas for shooting to wound Cecil Baker. The prosecuting attorneys wouldn't touch the case. They said it was a no-brainer, even with Thomas and Scout on probation.

Father Malcolm Dykstra's funeral is tomorrow morning at St. John the Baptist Catholic Church. Allie says we're all going, and none of us dare argue with her.

✖ ✖

I go over to Scout's Last Chance, to meet Joe and Allie for a bike ride. With Scout's bar broom, I sweep away the last remnants of bottle rockets and firecrackers from the steps. Then Joe pulls up, leans his bike against the building, Peapod wags without getting up, and we sprawl in the shade on the front step with Peapod while we wait for Allie.

Joe grins at me. "How ya doin' after all this, Sadie-Sadie?"

I smile back. "It feels good to just *be*."

Joe puts his hand on my knee. His touch sends a jolt of electricity through my legs and upward.

I say, "I'm glad it's over."

He looks into my eyes, like he can see all the way inside, and nods. "I feel about ten years older than I was six months ago, before John died."

I take his hand, the one that's on my knee, and we both squeeze.

"I sure am glad," he says, "that if I had to go through all this, it was with you."

I bite my lip. "Me too."

He leans closer and I feel his lips on mine before I realize that's what he's aiming for. His lips are soft, a tiny bit dry, but kind against mine. It feels good, and the electricity from the touch on the knee jerks to life and shoots all through me. I close my eyes and kiss him back, and

I feel warm all over, and I mean *all* over. Every time he kisses me, I feel like I could melt right into him.

"Sadie-Sadie," he says, pulling his mouth far enough away to talk. He leans his forehead against mine. "Finally. Whenever I try to kiss you, something else in our world goes haywire."

"Well, there's always now," I say. "What else can happen?"

Near our heads, Peapod starts a low-throttled growl, like an engine idling. We've grown to trust his growl, so we sit bolt upright before we hear the motor and before the dark blue pickup comes careening into the parking lot, spraying our legs with gravel.

"That," Joe says, "is what could happen."

The two jerks in the blue pickup, flags flying, have skidded to a gravelly stop right in front of us. Peapod is on his feet, his growl revved to full-throttle now.

"So you kids had to stick your noses where they didn't belong, didn't you," says the redneck with the Schlitz cap and the watery eyes. "Got Cecil Baker in the joint again."

"Cecil Baker got *himself* in the joint," Joe points out.

"And Miss High-and-Mighty Allison didn't do what her daddy said, and her puppy ended up dead."

"Shut up," I say, jumping up. "Just shut up about that. *YOU* killed her dog as much as Cecil did. You drugged him!"

"Well, he was a vicious thing, now wasn't he? And Cecil said we had to go git him, whatever it took."

The greasy ponytail guy's reptilian eyes narrow. I know this guy is dangerous, but he's just been a puppet for Cecil, and he's too stupid to be a threat without Cecil backing him up. After all we've been through, these two aren't so scary.

He says, "People 'round here don't like nosey people. You better start keepin' your nose in your own business. I'll bet you kids took my chain saw, too, didn't you? All the times you're ridin' around in them woods? I bet you took it to sell—"

"Your *chain saw?*" I almost choke.

Joe stares at the guy. "Now tell me. How exactly would we take a chain saw while we're riding bikes?"

"You watch your mouth, boy," the watery-eyed one says, spitting out the words.

"Is your name Steve Olsen?" I ask the ponytail guy.

"You *did* take it, didn'tcha?" He squints at me and spits tobacco sideways out his window.

"No," I say, choking back my desire to burst out laughing, amazed at how calm I can be. "But I saw your sign. I've been keeping an eye out for your saw. Haven't seen it in the woods, though."

"Think you're smart, don'tcha?" Droplets of saliva fly when the driver talks. "You watch yourselves."

We shake our heads and watch them peel out of the parking lot. The pickup tailgate and its *XXFUN* license plate disappear down the gravel road toward the trailer court.

"There you go," Joe says. "All I have to do is *touch* you and something happens. Maybe I should give up."

"I don't think so. Where were we?" I lean toward him, start the kiss myself. I press into him and he pulls me closer.

When we stop, Joe looks around. Nothing has exploded and nobody else has driven up.

"Hey," he says. "We did it."

"Yeah, we did."

We lie back on the cool cement, Joe's arm under my neck, him stroking my jawline with his finger, and we're quiet. I rub Peapod's rib cage from this almost-upside-down position.

"So you really will be my girlfriend?" Joe asks again. He takes my hand that isn't rubbing Peapod.

"I guess," I say.

"You guess?" He sits up, looking wounded.

"Joe, I mean I like you so much I can hardly stand it, but you're gonna be in Arizona and I'm gonna be in Minnesota."

"I'll see you in November," he says. "And we have half a summer left to figure it out."

"Okay," I say. "We can figure."

"I had a girlfriend," he tells me. "When John died, I mean. But I sort of ignored her. I hurt so bad, I felt dead. So we basically fell apart. Never broke up. Just *stopped*."

"Kind of like Father Malcolm's heart."

He half smiles, and touches my cheek with the back of his fingers. "But now," he says, "I know I'm alive again."

He takes my hand just as Allie comes around the corner.

"Hey!" She rolls up and brakes hard, spraying us with gravel almost like the truck did. Joe lets go of my hand, but not too quickly. Peapod jumps to his feet and wags his way over to her, delighted to see one of his favorite humans, licks her hand, then returns to the cement.

"So what's this?" she asks, nodding in the direction of our hand-holding. "Wow. I didn't know. When did this start?"

"Oh, AllieCat," I say, knowing my face is bright red. "On the Fourth of July, I guess. Or when we didn't know where you were. Never really had a chance to start before this. It's been sort of a crazy week." I squint at her because the sun is behind her back, streaming down and glistening off her tanned shoulder muscles. I try to read her face to see if she's pissed or sad or jealous or just surprised that I'm with Joe and not with her. I didn't mean to flaunt it, 'cause she doesn't need anything else to be sad right now. I don't know how to do this—I've never been the one in the middle that two people wanted. But Allie grins at me and I know it's okay.

"Mostly," I add, "we're just busy not being dead."

"Funny how close we are to getting ourselves dead any old time, isn't it?" Allie shakes her head. "Life's pretty fragile, and you can just *stop being*, can't you?"

I think about Father Malcolm's heart—just stopping. About Siren overheating, having a seizure, and ending up dead. About Joe's brother John exploding on the canyon floor. Alive one minute, dead the next. And Scout taking a bullet in his bone and living.

And we're alive.

We're quiet again. We're good at being quiet together.

"So—" Allie lifts her handlebars and lets her front wheel bounce on its shock. "Are we gonna ride, or are you two lovebirds too busy necking?"

"Shut up, Allie," I say. "Of course we're riding."

"Or," Allie says, "should we just sit here and be amazed at being alive?"

"Come on, you AllieCat." Joe grins and jumps to his feet. "Isn't that kind of why we ride?"

Straddling her bike's top tube, Allie takes her helmet off, shakes her spiky hair, and runs her hands through it to make it stand on end. "Guess so. I hadn't thought of it that way. But yeah, every time we don't kill ourselves on some hill, we're still alive. That rush is about as alive as you get, I guess."

"Hey, Allie," I say, picking up my bike. "You want to move to Minnetonka with me? Want to come live with us?

We've got room. You could ride with me on Buck Hill, and we could come stay with Scout in the summer. Want to? I can ask my mom. But I know she'll say yes."

Allie fingers her helmet fastener. She looks at the sky, so deep blue you can get lost looking into it, and then she looks toward the junk woods, the place where Siren is buried. She gives me half a smile, and I know and she knows that I would never offer if I weren't completely comfortable with her, even though she kissed me.

"Thanks, Sadie. But no thanks. I belong here. And Siren might come lookin' for me. His ghost wouldn't know what to do in that traffic."

"Allie, you're not serious about being stuck here 'cause of a dead dog, are you?" Joe asks. "You're not just saying that 'cause you're chicken to move?"

"Naw." Allie slides her helmet back on. "But I do belong here. I need to keep an eye on my mom when she gets out. They're letting me stay with her since I'm sixteen and she'll only be in day treatment. And then they got us doing some kind of family counseling. Like that'll help." She rolls her eyes. "But I'll do it. And somebody has to keep Scout from blowing up the neighborhood. So I guess the chicken I gotta ride through is right here." She grins at both of us. "We all got our own chicken, don't we?" She fastens her helmet. "Plus, Mike told me at the bike shop that he knows somebody who needs to find homes for some puppies … some little dog needs me."

I grin at her. So does Joe.

"I just belong here, okay?" she says, sweeping her hand across the river, the valley, and the junk woods. "So, let's shut up and ride."

Then we're on our bikes. We're flying down the hill, through the junk woods, toward the Blue Earth River, trees streaking past us, sun beating on our shoulders, wind in our faces.

And we are alive.